# The
# Mistletoe
# Promise

Center Point
Large Print

Also by Richard Paul Evans and available from Center Point Large Print:

*A Step of Faith*
*Walking on Water*

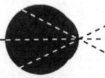

# The Mistletoe Promise

## Richard Paul Evans

CENTER POINT LARGE PRINT
THORNDIKE, MAINE

This Center Point Large Print edition is published in the year 2015 by arrangement with Simon & Schuster, Inc.

The text of this Large Print edition is unabridged.
In other aspects, this book may vary
from the original edition.
Printed in the United States of America
on permanent paper.
Set in 16-point Times New Roman type.

ISBN: 978-1-62899-780-4

Library of Congress Cataloging-in-Publication Data

Evans, Richard Paul.
The mistletoe promise / Richard Paul Evans. —
    Center Point Large Print edition.
pages cm
ISBN 978-1-62899-780-4 (hardcover : alk. paper)
1. Large type books.  2. Christmas stories.  I. Title.
PS3555.V259M57 2015
813'.54—dc23
                                        2015032937

To Gypsy da Silva

Elise is a derivation of Elishaeva,
a Hebrew name meaning God's promise.

If you could erase just one day from your life, would you know the day? For some, a specific date comes to mind, one that lives in personal infamy. It may be the day you lost someone you love. Or it might be the time you did something you regret, a mistake you wish you could fix. It may be a combination of both.

I am one of those people who would know the day. There is one day that has brought me unspeakable pain, and the effects of that day continue to cover and erode my world like rust. I suspect that someday the rust will eat through the joists and posts of my life and I will topple, literally as well as figuratively.

I have punished myself for my mistake more times than I can remember. Each day I wake up in the court of conscience to be judged guilty and unworthy. In this sorry realm I am the judge, prosecutor, and jury, and, without defense, I accept the verdict and the sentence, a lifetime of regret and guilt to be administered by myself.

I'm not the only one who has punished me for

what I've done. Not by a long shot. The world has weighed in on my failure as well. Some people I know, more I don't. And there are those who have learned to use my mistake against me—to punish or control me. My ex-husband was an expert on wielding my mistake against me, and for too long I offered up no defense.

Then one day a man came along who was willing to plead my case. Not so ironically, he was an attorney. And, for the first time since that black day, I felt joy without the need to squash it. I met him around the holidays just a little more than a year ago. And that too is a day I'll never forget.

# Chapter One

*I'm not ready for another Christmas.
I haven't been since 2007.*

## Elise Dutton's Diary

### NOVEMBER 1, 2012

I hated the change; the commercial changing of the seasons was more obvious than nature's. It was November first, the day after Halloween, when orange and black gives way to red and green. I didn't always hate the change; I once looked forward to it. But that seemed like a lifetime ago.

I watched as the maintenance staff of the office building where I worked transformed the food court. A large, synthetic Christmas tree was dragged out to the middle of the room, strung with white lights, and draped in blue and silver tinsel. Giant corrugated-styrene snowflakes were brought out of storage and hung from the ceiling, just as they had been every year for as long as I'd worked in downtown Salt Lake City.

I was watching the transformation when I noticed him staring at me. *Him*—the stranger who would change everything. I didn't know his name, but I had seen him before. I'd probably seen him a hundred times before, as we ate pretty much every day in the same food court: I near the Cafe Rio with my sweet pork salad and he, fifty yards away, over by the Japanese food emporium eating something with chopsticks. *Why was he looking at me?*

He was handsome. Not in your Photoshopped Abercrombie & Fitch catalog way—women weren't necessarily stopping midsentence when he walked into a room—but he certainly did catch their attention. He was about six feet tall, trim, narrow-hipped, athletically built. He was always dressed impeccably—in an expensive, custom-tailored suit, with a crisp white shirt and a silk tie.

I guessed he was a lawyer and, from his accoutrements, one who made good money. I, on the other hand, worked as a hotel and venue coordinator at a midlevel travel wholesaler booking educational trips for high school students. The company I worked for was called the International Consortium of Education, but we all just called it by its acronym, ICE, which was appropriate as I felt pretty frozen in my job. I guess that was true of most of my life.

The lawyer and I had had eye contact before. It was two or three weeks back when I had stepped on an elevator that he was already on. The button for the seventh floor was lit, which was further evidence that he was a lawyer, since the top two floors of the tower were occupied by law firms.

He had smiled at me, and I'd given him an obligatory return smile. I remember his gaze had lingered on me a little longer than I'd expected, long enough to make me feel self-conscious. He'd looked at me as if he knew me, or wanted to say something, then he'd turned away. I thought he had stolen a glance at my bare ring finger, though later I decided that it had just been my imagination. I had gotten off the elevator on the third floor with another woman, who sighed, "He was gorgeous." I had nodded in agreement.

After that, the lawyer and I had run into each other dozens of times, each time offering the same obligatory smiles. But today he was staring at me. Then he got up and started across the room toward me, a violation of our unspoken relational agreement.

At first I thought he was walking toward me, then I thought he wasn't, which made me feel stupid, like when someone waves at you in a crowd and you're not sure who they are, but you wave back before realizing that they were waving at someone behind you. But then there he was, this gorgeous man, standing five feet in front of me, staring at me with my mouth full of salad.

"Hi," he said.

"Hi," I returned, swallowing insufficiently chewed lettuce.

"Do you mind if I join you?"

I hesitated. "No, it's okay."

As he sat down he reached across the table. "My name is Nicholas. Nicholas Derr. You can call me Nick."

"Hi, Nicholas," I said, subtly refusing his offer of titular intimacy. "I'm Elise."

"Elise," he echoed. "That's a pretty name."

"Thank you."

"Want to see something funny?"

Before I could answer, he unfolded a piece of paper from his coat pocket, then set it on the table in front of me. "A colleague of mine just showed these to me."

I know a guy who's addicted to brake fluid. He says he can stop anytime.

I didn't like my beard at first. Then it grew on me.

He pointed to the last one. "This is my favorite."

I stayed up all night to see where the sun went. Then it dawned on me.

"Is that what you do at work?" I asked.

"Pretty much. That and computer solitaire," he said, folding the paper back into his pocket. "How about you?"

"Candy Crush."

"I mean, where do you work?"

"On the third floor of the tower. It's a travel company."

"What's it called?"

"I.C.E."

"Ice?"

"It stands for International Consortium of Education."

"What kind of travel do you do?"

"We arrange educational tours for high school students to historic sites, like Colonial Williamsburg or Philadelphia or New York. Teachers sign up their classes."

"I wouldn't think there was a lot of travel on a teacher's salary."

"That's the point," I said. "If they get enough of their students signed up, they come along free as chaperones."

"Ah, it's a racket."

"Basically. Let me guess, you're a lawyer."

"How could you tell?"

"You look like one. What's your firm?"

"Derr, Nelson and McKay."

"That's a mouthful," I said. "Speaking of which, do you mind if I finish eating before my salad gets cold?"

He cocked his head. "Isn't salad supposed to be cold?"

"Not the meat. It's sweet pork."

"No, please eat." He leaned back a little while I ate, surveying the room. "Looks like the holiday assault force has landed. I wish they would take a break this year. The holidays depress me."

"Why is that?"

"Because it's lonely just watching others celebrate."

It was exactly how I felt. "I know what you mean."

"I thought you might."

"Why do you say that?"

"I just noticed that you usually eat alone."

I immediately went on the defensive. "It's only because my workmates and I take different lunch-times to watch the phones."

He frowned. "I didn't mean to offend you. I'm just saying that I've noticed we've both spent a lot of time down here alone."

"I didn't notice," I lied.

He looked into my eyes. "So you're probably wondering what I want."

"It's crossed my mind."

"It's taken me a few days to get up the courage

to come over here and talk to you, which is saying something, since I'm not afraid of much." He hesitated for a moment, as if gathering his thoughts. "The first time I saw you I thought, *Why is such a beautiful woman sitting there alone?* Then I saw you the next day, and the next day . . ."

"Your point?" I said.

"My point is, I'm tired of being alone during the holidays. I'm tired of walking through holiday crowds of humanity feeling like a social leper." He looked into my eyes. "Are you?"

"Am I what?"

"Tired of being alone during the holidays."

I shook my head. "No, I'm good."

He looked surprised. "Really?"

"Really."

He looked surprised *and* a little deflated. "Oh," he said, looking down as if thinking. Then he looked back up at me and forced a smile. "Good, then. That's good for you. I'm glad you're happy." He stood. "Well, Elise, it was a pleasure to finally meet you. I'm sorry to bother you. Enjoy your salad and have a nice holiday." He turned to leave.

"Wait a second," I said. "Where are you going?"

"Back to work."

"Why did you come over here?"

"It's not important."

"It was important enough for you to cross the food court."

"It *was* important. Now it's moot."

"Moot?" I said. "Sit down. Tell me what's moot."

He looked at me for a moment, then sat back down. "I just thought that maybe you felt the same way about the holidays as I do, but since you're *good,* you clearly don't. So what I was going to say is now moot."

I looked at him a moment, then said, "I might have exaggerated my contentment. So what were you going to say that is now moot?"

"I had a proposition to make."

"Right here in the food court?"

"We could go to my office if you prefer."

"No, here in public is good."

"I'll cut to the chase. Socially, this is a busy time of year for me. And, like I said, I'm tired of being alone during the holidays, going to all my company and client dinners and parties alone, enduring everyone's sympathy and answering everyone's questions about why a successful, nice-looking attorney is still single. And, for the sake of argument, we'll say that you're also tired of doing the holidays solo."

"Go on," I said.

"As one who would rather light a candle than curse the darkness, I say that we do something about it. What I'm proposing is a mutually beneficial holiday arrangement. For the next eight weeks we are, for all intents and purposes, a couple."

I looked at him blankly. "Are you kidding me?"

"Think about it," he said. "It's the perfect solution. We don't know each other, so there's no deep stuff, no pain, no bickering. The only commitment is to be good to each other and to be good company."

"And being good company means ending up back at your place?"

"No, I'm proposing a purely platonic relationship. Maybe we publicly hold hands now and then to sell the facade, but that's the extent of our physicality."

I shook my head skeptically. "Men can't have platonic relationships."

"In real life, you're probably right. But this isn't real life. It's fiction. And it's just until Christmas."

"How do I know you're not a serial killer?"

He laughed. "You don't. You could ask my ex, but no one's found the body."

"What?"

"Just kidding. I've never been married."

"You're serious about this?"

He nodded. "Completely."

"I think you're crazy."

"Maybe. Or maybe I'm a genius and everyone will be doing this in the future."

I slowly shook my head, not sure of what to think of the proposal or the proposer.

"Look, I know it's unconventional, but oftentimes the best solutions are. Will you at least consider it?"

I looked at him for a moment, then said, "All right. I'll think about it. No guarantees. Probably not."

"Fair enough," he said, standing. "I'm leaving town tonight, but I'll be back Monday."

"That will give me some time to think about it," I said.

"I eagerly await your response."

"Don't be too eager," I said.

"It's been a pleasure, Elise." He smiled as he turned and walked away.

# Chapter Two

*Often what we see clearest in others
is what we most avoid seeing in ourselves.*

## ELISE DUTTON'S DIARY

The encounter left me a little dazed. I didn't tell anyone about it. Actually, I didn't really have anyone to tell. The person at work I spent the most time with was my colleague Zoey, and I definitely wouldn't be telling her. You don't know Zoey, but you do. Every company, every school in the world has a Zoey—the kind of girl who attracts male attention like a porch light attracts moths. She was naturally beautiful, skinny without starving or Zumba, born with a body that designers design for. She even looked good without makeup, which I knew for a fact since she usually spent the first hour at work applying it.

Even worse than being beautiful was that she knew it. A few months after I started at ICE, before I really even knew her, she offered to give me some makeup, which sounded like her saying that I could be pretty if I tried. I think what hurt the most about her offer was that, whether she meant to convey that message or not, it was true. I didn't take care of myself. After Dan, my ex-husband, divorced me, I just sort of let things slide. Not completely, but enough to change. I put on a little weight, and stopped spending time at the mirror or buying clothes. I guess I was treating myself the way I felt—undesirable.

At the opposite extreme, Zoey was in her prime with a perpetually full roster of men, with someone always up to bat and someone always on deck, ready to fill in when she tired of the current player. She was the one our company's airline and hotel reps, mostly balding, middle-aged men, would plan their office visits around. I worked a trade show with her once, and the whole time men circled our booth like vultures over carrion. Zoey ate it up. Why wouldn't she?

What I had said to the lawyer about eating alone at lunch was true, mostly. One of us was supposed to watch the phones, but that's what voice mail is for, right? The real reason I hated to eat lunch with Zoey was because all I ended up doing was politely listening to her myriad stories of affairs and conquests while I sat there feeling frumpy and old. It's easy to hate the game when you're losing.

# *Chapter Three*

*I can't believe that I'm actually
considering this man's proposal.
Am I crazy, desperate or just really
lonely? Probably all of the above.*

## ELISE DUTTON'S DIARY

That weekend, all I could think about was the proposition. *Who was this guy and what did he want? What was his motive?* I suppose, on a deeper level, the bigger question (considering how lonely I was) was *Why was I even questioning his motive?* Why couldn't he be exactly what he claimed to be? Was that really so hard to accept?

My father used to say, "If it ain't broke, don't fix it—but if it's already broke, it don't matter what you do." My life was definitely broken. So why not? Really, what did I have to lose? I even asked myself, *What would Zoey do?* I knew what she'd do. She'd say, "You only live once, girl," and she'd buckle up for the ride. I suppose that my mind was probably somewhere in Zoeyland when I decided to say yes.

• • •

The next Monday, Nicholas arrived in the food court about a half hour after I'd started eating.

"Hi, Elise," he said. "How's your salad?"

"Good."

"How was your weekend?"

"The usual," I said, even though it was definitely anything but.

He sat down across from me. "Did you come to a decision?"

"Right to the point," I said. I set down my plastic fork. "So, hypothetically, let's say that I said yes. What would this arrangement look like?"

He smiled. "First, we write up a contract."

"Why, you don't trust me?"

"Contracts are not always so much a matter of trust as they are a matter of understanding. This way we'll be more likely to meet each other's expectations."

*I should have had one of those before my marriage,* I thought.

He leaned in closer. "Let me tell you what I had in mind. I'll pay for all meals, transportation, and admissions. We'll have lunch together when possible and, in addition to the social functions, I'll take you to dinner or some holiday-themed event at least once a week, and I'll send you something, a gift, each weekday up until the end of the contract. Then, at midnight on Christmas Eve, the agreement terminates and we go back to our lonely, pathetic lives."

"If I agree, how do we start?"

"We'll begin by going through each other's calendars and determining what events we can attend. It's two-sided, of course. If you'd like, I'll attend your events as well."

I thought a moment more, then, with his eyes locked onto mine, said, "All right."

"All right, let's do it?" he asked.

I nodded. "Yes. Let's do it."

"Are you sure?"

"Why not? Lunch every day?"

"When possible. At least every workday. We're two days in on that now. It hasn't been too painful, has it?"

"It's definitely been interesting. I don't know about you sending me things."

"Why?"

I shrugged. "I don't know."

"You'll get used to it."

"Do I have to send you things too?"

"No. I expect nothing but the pleasure of your company."

I took a deep breath. "Okay. Get me a contract."

"Great," he said, standing. "I'll see you tomorrow."

"You're not having lunch?"

"No. I have a deposition in an hour that I still

need to prepare for. I just came down to see you."

Something about the way he said that pleased me. "All right, I'll see you tomorrow."

"Thank you, Elise. I don't think you'll regret it."

A minute later, a food court worker said to me, "You have a cute husband."

"He's not my husband," I said. "He's . . ." I paused. "He's my boyfriend."

"Lucky you," she said.

# Chapter Four

*I'm not sure what I've gotten myself into with this contract, but I'm still looking for the fine print.*

## ELISE DUTTON'S DIARY

The next day Nicholas walked into the food court carrying a leather Coach briefcase. I was sitting at my usual table, waiting for him. He smiled when he saw me. "Shall we eat at Cafe Rio?" he asked.

"Sure," I said.

We walked together up to the restaurant's counter. "I've never eaten here before," he said. "What's good?"

"The sweet pork salad is pretty much my mainstay," I said.

"Two sweet pork salads," Nicholas said to the woman who was rolling out tortillas.

"Pinto beans or black beans?" she asked.

Nicholas deferred to me. "I didn't realize there would be a quiz. I'll let you take over."

"Pinto beans," I said. "With the house dressing. Cheese, no pico."

"I'll have the same," he said.

"Drink?"

"The sugar-free lemonade," I said.

"One sugar-free lemonade and a Coke," Nicholas said.

He paid for our meals, then, while I got our drinks, he carried our tray over to a table.

"This is pretty good," he said. "I can see why you have it every day."

"It may be the most delicious salad ever made," I replied.

After we had eaten for a few minutes, he reached into his briefcase and brought out some documents. "Here you go," he said, holding out the papers. "The contract."

"This looks so *official*."

"It's what I do," he said.

I looked it over.

## MISTLETOE CONTRACT

"Why mistletoe?"

"You know how, at Christmastime, people show affection under mistletoe to people they're not necessarily affectionate with?"

"That's clever," I said. "Can we change the word *contract?* It sounds too . . . formal."

"What would you prefer?"

I thought a moment. "How about *promise?*"

"Done," he said, striking a line through the word *contract* and penning in the rest. "The Mistletoe Promise."

I looked over the agreement.

MISTLETOE ~~CONTRACT~~ PROMISE
This service agreement is made effective as of November 6th by and between

Elise Dutton (Lessor) and Nicholas Derr (Lessee).

"How did you know my last name?"

"I'm a lawyer," he said, which didn't really answer my question.

1. DESCRIPTION OF SERVICES.
Lessor will exert due effort to provide to Lessee the following services (collectively, the "Services"):
   a. Lunch together each weekday as individual schedules permit.
   b. At least one evening activity per week through duration of contract.
   c. Best effort to demonstrate a caring relationship.

I couldn't help but think how every relationship would benefit from such an agreement.

2. PAYMENT. In consideration of Lessor's services, Lessee agrees to pay for all dinners, joint activities, admission fees, travel expenses, etc., for the duration of Contract.

"Travel expenses?" I asked.
"Gas money," he said. "Mostly."

If Lessee fails to pay for the Services when due, Lessor has the option to treat such failure to pay as a material breach of this Contract, and may cancel this Contract but not seek legal redress.

3. TERM. This agreement will terminate automatically on December 24, 2012, at 11:59:59 p.m.

4. LANGUAGE. Lessor and Lessee shall, for the duration of this agreement, refer to each other as *boyfriend* or *girlfriend* or by any term of endearment including, but not limited to, *sweetie, sweetheart, love, dear, babe, beautiful, cupcake,* and any term found acceptable by both parties.

I looked at him incredulously. "Really? *Cupcake?*"
"I wasn't planning on using *cupcake.*"
"Then why did you put it in the contract?"
"In case you were. It's just an example," he

said. "Granted a poor one. But I don't know your preferences."

"I would rather not be called after any food or animal. Actually, avoid any noun."

"Consider all nouns, especially *cupcake,* stricken from my vocabulary. Does that include *honey?*"

I thought about it. "I guess *honey* is okay. It's gone mainstream."

"*Honey,* okay," he said to himself.

I went back to the contract.

5. PLATONIC NATURE OF ARRANGE-MENT. This agreement does not constitute, imply, or encourage, directly or indirectly, a physical relationship, other than what would be considered expected and appropriate public physical contact.

"What does that mean? *Expected* physical contact."

"Nothing exciting," he said. "Hand-holding in public, that sort of thing." When I didn't respond he added, "Things real couples do. For instance, we might hold hands at a company party, at least when walking into the party, but we wouldn't be holding hands when we are alone, since that obviously wouldn't be necessary to convince others."

"I get it," I said.

6. CONFIDENTIALITY. Lessor and her agents will not at any time or in any manner,

either directly or indirectly, divulge, disclose, or communicate in any manner, any information that is proprietary to this agreement and agrees to protect such information and treat it as strictly confidential. This provision will continue to be effective until the termination of this Contract.

7. BREACH OF CONTRACT. If any of the above stipulations are not met, Contract will be considered null and void. No recourse is available.

ADDENDUMS
1. No deep, probing personal questions.
2. No drama.

"Talk to me about these addendums."

"The first is self-explanatory. We do not ask each other any deep, probing personal questions. It's irrelevant to our objective and will only cause problems. Do you really want me asking deep personal questions about your life and past?"

I tried to hide the effect the question had on me. "Nope, I'm good."

"Exactly. This relationship should be so shallow there's no possibility of drowning."

"Agreed," I said. "And the second?"

"No drama. Life's too short."

"Agreed."

"Then all that's left is your signature."

I looked at the signatory line. He had already signed the contract. "Why do I feel like I'm signing away my soul?"

"It's not an eternity. Just forty-nine days."

I breathed out. "All right. Do you have a pen?"

"I'm a lawyer. That's like asking me if I have a lung."

"As opposed to a heart," I said.

"Another fan of lawyers," he said. He extracted a pen from his coat pocket. It was a nice one—a Montblanc. I knew this only because my ex judged a man by the pen he carried. I took the pen from Nicholas and signed the document.

"There are two copies," he said. "One for your own files. Please sign both."

"Now you're really sounding like a lawyer."

"I am one."

"So you keep reminding me." I folded the contract in half and put it in my purse.

When I'd finished eating my salad I said, "I better get back to work."

"I'll walk you to the elevator," he said. As we waited for the elevator he said, "Don't forget to bring your calendar tomorrow so we can work out our schedule."

"I'll be ready."

As the elevator door opened he leaned forward and kissed my cheek. "Have a good day, dear."

"Thanks for lunch," I said. *"Cupcake."*

He smiled. "This is going to be fun."

# Chapter Five

*Bad memories can attach themselves
like barnacles to the hulls of our lives.
And, like barnacles, they have a
disproportionately large amount of drag.*

### ELISE DUTTON'S DIARY

Zoey screamed. Cathy, our company bookkeeper, and I rushed out of our offices to see a florist deliveryman standing in the middle of the office holding a massive bouquet of yellow roses. It was one of the largest bouquets I'd ever seen, the kind people were more likely to send to the dead than the living. Of course the man was drooling over Zoey.

"They're gorgeous," Cathy said. "Who are they from?"

"I don't know," Zoey said. "Probably Paul. Or Quentin. Could even be Brody. So many men, so many possibilities."

I rolled my eyes at her theatrics.

"Where would you like them?" the man asked.

"Oh, just set them there," Zoey said, motioning to her desk. "It practically takes up my whole desk."

"And if I could have you sign right here." He handed Zoey an electronic clipboard. Her expression abruptly changed. "They're not for me." She looked up at me. "They're for you."

"Elise?" Cathy said, not masking her surprise.

Just then Mark, our boss, walked into the room.

"Those are pretty . . . massive," he said, looking at Zoey. "Who now?"

"They're not for me," Zoey said. "They're for Elise."

He looked at me. "Someone's got a fever for you."

I walked over to my flowers. There was a small, unsealed envelope attached to the vase. I extracted the card.

*Dear Elise,*
*Happy Day 1. I hope the*
*flowers brighten your day.*
*—Nick*

"Who are they from?" Cathy asked.

I looked back up at them. "What?"

"Who gave them to you?"

"Just . . . a guy."

"What guy?" Zoey asked.

"My *boyfriend*." The word came out awkwardly.

35

They both looked at me with expressions of bewilderment.

"You have a boyfriend?" Zoey asked.

"It's new," I said. I lifted the heavy vase and carried it to my office. *Thank you, thank you, thank you,* I thought. I couldn't wait to thank Nicholas.

Flowers are complicated. The last time I had received flowers from a man was a nightmare. I was in the hospital and I'd just come out of intensive care after almost dying from a burst appendix, but the pain I remember most wasn't caused by the operation. It was caused by my husband. But I'll share more of that later.

I debated over whether or not I should take the flowers home, but finally decided to leave them at the office. I told myself that they were so big I doubted I could get them into my apartment without damaging them. But really I think I left them in the office in defiance of my co-workers' incredulity. Driving home, all I could think about was that it had been the best day I'd had in a long time.

The next morning at work I was making copies of a travel itinerary for a group of high school students from Boise, Idaho, when I heard Zoey greet someone.

"I have a delivery for Elise Dutton," a man said.

I walked out of my office. "That would be me."

"Here you go," the man said, handing me a box.

"What is it?" Zoey asked.

"I don't know," I said. "It's wrapped." I opened the box and smiled. "Oh. Chocolate cordials." I wondered how he knew that I loved them. There was a card.

*Happy Day 2, Elise. So far so good?*
*—Nick*

"What are cordials?" Zoey asked.

"Chocolate-covered cherries," I said.

"Why don't they just call them chocolate-covered cherries?"

"Because they're cordials," I replied. I took one out and popped it into my mouth. It was delicious. "Want one?"

"Sure." She looked a little injured as she walked over to me. "Tell me more about this guy."

Even though it was the first time she'd ever asked me about my personal life, I didn't want to share. "He's really just more of a friend," I said.

"Guys don't send chocolates and massive flower bouquets just to be friends. There's always an agenda. What's the lowdown?"

"His name is Nicholas."

"What does he do?"

"He's a lawyer on the seventh floor."

"Nicholas what?"

"Derr."

She puzzled a moment then said, "As in Derr, Nelson and McKay? You're dating one of the partners?"

"We're just . . ." The truth was, I didn't know whether or not he was a partner, but Zoey's incredulity made me angry. "Yes. Of course."

"Oh," she said. "Well done."

"Don't look so surprised," I said.

"It's just that you've never showed much interest in dating."

"Maybe I just hadn't met the right man," I replied.

"Nicholas is the right man?"

"Maybe." This was already more fun than I'd thought it would be. "I've decided to at least give him until Christmas."

"You're giving *him* until Christmas?"

"I think that's enough time to see if I like him."

She looked almost stunned. "Okay," she said. She started to turn away, then said, "Oh, could you trade me lunchtimes today? I met this guy last night and he's coming to meet me."

"I'm sorry," I said. "I'm meeting Nicholas."

You have no idea how good it felt saying no. It was the first time I'd ever turned her down. It was the first time I'd had a reason to.

A little after noon I went to the food court. Nicholas wasn't there yet, so I ordered my usual salad and sat down at my usual table. Nicholas showed up about ten minutes later.

"I'm sorry I'm late," he said, looking stressed. "Long-winded client, antitrust stuff. Too dull to discuss."

"It's okay," I said.

He sat down across from me. "How's your day?"

"Good," I said. "Thank you for the flowers. They're beautiful."

"Like you."

I smiled a little. "And the chocolates."

"Do you like chocolate?"

"All women like chocolate. It's like female catnip."

He grinned. "I hoped as much."

"You don't need to spend so much, you know."

"I know," he said simply.

"Are you going to get something to eat?"

"No, I'm sorry. I know we were going to go through our schedules today, but my morning fell apart and I have to get back to that meeting. I just didn't want to leave you hanging down here alone."

"It's okay, I'm used to it."

"You shouldn't be," he said. "Is tomorrow okay?"

"Same time, same place."

"Thanks. I'll see you tomorrow. Bye, Elise."

"Bye."

He got up and walked away.

Maybe it was a small thing, but the fact that in spite of his busy schedule Nicholas had come down to meet me meant even more than the flowers and chocolates.

Back when I was still married, my husband, Dan, invited me to lunch, then forgot about it. I waited alone for almost an hour before calling him.

"Sorry, I forgot," he said. "I got distracted."

"Am I that forgettable?" I asked.

"Don't talk to me about *forgetting*," he said.

That shut me up. I hung up the phone, then broke down crying.

I finished my lunch and went back to work.

# *Chapter Six*

*The lawyer and I made our plans for the next seven weeks. It looks like fun. Which is probably what the last Hindenburg passenger thought as he boarded the blimp.*

## ELISE DUTTON'S DIARY

The next morning I was booking rooms at a New York hotel when Zoey walked in carrying a silver box from Nordstrom and set it on my desk.

"It's from the lawyer," she whispered. Then she just stood there, waiting for me to finish the call. As soon as I hung up she said, "Open it." She looked even more eager to see what was inside the box than I was. I opened the card first.

*Day 3. It's been a cold winter, Elise. I thought this might help.*
*—Nick*

"So what did Lover Boy send today?" Zoey asked, sounding incredibly jealous. I'd be lying if I said that I didn't enjoy it.

"Let's find out," I said. I untied the ribbon, then lifted the lid. Inside was a piece of light tan cloth. I lifted it out.

"It's a scarf," I said. "It's soft."

Zoey touched it. "It's cashmere." She instinctively went for the label. "Pashmina from Bottega Veneta." She looked up at me. "You realize that's like six hundred dollars."

I tried not to look impressed. "Really?"

"This guy's made of money. What does he drive?"

"I don't know."

"How do you not know?"

"I haven't been out with him yet."

"Amazing," she said, shaking her head as she walked out of my office.

I wore the scarf to lunch. Nicholas was waiting for me near Cafe Rio. He stood, smiling, as I approached. "I see you got it," he said, looking at the scarf.

"What did I say about spending so much?"

"You told me I didn't have to, which I already knew."

"I feel uncomfortable."

"Why?"

"I don't know."

"Then don't worry about it. I don't expect reciprocity, so you don't need to worry about anything. Just enjoy it." He looked into my eyes. "Or at least let me enjoy it, okay?"

"Okay. Thank you. It's beautiful."

"It's cashmere," he said.

"I know. Zoey told me. She's insanely jealous."

"Is a jealous Zoey a good or bad thing?"

"That depends on who you ask."

"I'm asking you."

"Definitely a good thing."

He smiled. "What are we eating today? Cafe Rio again?"

"Of course."

"I should have just ordered for you. Before this is over I'm going to expand your culinary horizons. Save our place and I'll be right back. Sweet pork salad, pinto beans, house dressing."

"And a diet lemonade."

"Of course."

Not wanting to get food on my scarf, I folded it up and stowed it in my purse. Nicholas returned a few minutes later carrying a tray. "One salad with lots of sugar, and a lemonade sans sugar."

"Thank you."

He sat down.

"What did you get?" I asked, examining his meal.

"I thought I'd try the chiles rellenos with some of this rice." He took a bite, then asked, "Who is this Zoey person?"

"She's just someone I work with." A peculiar feeling swept through me. I didn't want him to know who Zoey was. I didn't want him to meet her. I didn't want her to take him. "She's, like, beautiful."

"Like you," he said.

"No, she's *really* beautiful."

His expression immediately changed. He almost looked angry. "As opposed to what?"

"As opposed to me."

He leaned back for a moment, then said, "How long have you been this way?"

"What way?"

"Self-deprecating."

Suddenly, to my surprise, tears began to well up in my eyes. I didn't answer. I was too embarrassed.

He didn't back off. "What makes you think you're not beautiful?"

"I'm not blind," I said. "I can look in a mirror."

"You have a flawed mirror," he replied. His voice softened. "Elise, anyone can open a book. Not everyone can appreciate the beauty of the writing. I want you to stop berating yourself."

"It's just . . ." I wiped my eyes with a napkin. "Around my office I'm not the one who gets the flowers."

"Funny," he said. "I could have sworn you told me that you just got some."

*What was this man doing to me?* "Can we just eat?"

"I want to add something to our contract. For

44

the length of our agreement you will believe that you are beautiful."

"You can't just change a belief."

"People do it all the time," he said. "Besides, it's contractual. You don't have a choice. You'd be amazed at what people accomplish under contract."

"I don't know if I can do that."

"Then at least believe that I believe you're beautiful."

I sat there fighting back tears. "Can we please change the subject?"

"Will you agree to do this one thing for me?"

Finally I nodded.

"All right. Now we can eat."

We ate for a few minutes until he said, "I'm going to run out of time, so we'd better start planning our season." He reached into his briefcase and brought out some papers. "I had my secretary print out copies of my calendar for the next two months. We can use it to plan."

He handed me two pages, and I quickly looked through the calendar. Not surprisingly, he had a lot more going on than I did. I didn't need a secretary to schedule my life. I didn't even need a notebook.

"You have two work parties," I noted.

"Yes, I'm sorry if that's excessive. There's an office party for the entire firm, then there's the partners' party."

"Gee, I wonder which one is nicer," I said.

"Actually, they're both nice," he said. "The company party is at La Caille."

"Really?" La Caille was an expensive French restaurant in the foothills of the Wasatch Mountains. "That's nice."

"You've been there?"

"It's been a few years. Actually, I was there for a wedding. It's a bit above my pay grade. Where's the partners' party, the Grand America?"

"The partners' party is at one of our founders' homes."

I went back to the beginning of the calendar. The first event Nicholas had marked was the evening of November ninth. Tomorrow night.

"What's this Hale Centre event?" I asked.

"That's the Hale Centre Theatre's production of *A Christmas Carol*. I've heard it's great, I've just never wanted to go alone." He looked at me. "I know it's sudden. If you have other plans . . ."

"No, it's okay," I said. "I'm not busy."

He looked pleased.

I moved down the calendar. "What about the following weekend? You marked an event on the sixteenth."

"There's nothing scheduled, but is there something you would like to do? We could go to the symphony, ballet, Walmart . . ."

"Let me think about it," I said. I moved my

finger to the next week on the calendar. "The next week is Thanksgiving."

"Thanksgiving is early this year. Do you have plans?"

"I usually spend it with Dan's family."

"Who's Dan?"

"My ex."

He looked at me quizzically. "Really?"

"I know, it's weird. But I'm still close to his parents. The way they see it, their son divorced me but they didn't. I think they like me more than they like him."

"How does your ex feel about it?"

"He's strangely good with it. In a twisted way I think it makes him feel like he has a harem."

"That's creepy."

"That would describe him."

"You don't have a better alternative? Family?"

"There's no one close. My parents have both passed away. I have a sister in Minneapolis. She invites me to her house every year, but it's too expensive to fly there for a day."

"You don't get frequent-flier miles with the travel agency?" he asked. Then he answered his own question. "I guess you couldn't use them on Thanksgiving anyway. It's a blackout period."

"I don't get them. I don't travel with the groups. We have people who do that. I just do the logistics, like booking hotels and admissions at some of the venues."

He nodded as he took this all in. "So, back to Thanksgiving at your ex's family. I assume Dan and company wouldn't like me joining them. Disrupt the harem and all that."

"No, that might be awkward."

"Then would you be willing to join me?"

"With your family?"

"No, in that department we're in the same boat. I celebrate Thanksgiving with the family of one of the attorneys I work with."

"What's their name?"

"The Hitesmans," he said. "Scott Hitesman. Real nice family."

I wrote the name down on the calendar.

"Scott joined the firm about the same time I did. We were working over a Thanksgiving weekend on a big case, and he invited me to join them. I've been with them ever since."

"Will they be okay if I come?"

Nicholas laughed. "No, they'll be *ecstatic*. Sharon is always trying to get me to invite someone."

"Then it's a date. Will I need to bring anything?"

"I usually just pick up some pies from Marie Callender's."

"I can make pie," I said. "I like baking. I make a pumpkin pie that's to die for. And a pecan pie that's at least worth getting sick for."

He grimaced.

"That didn't come out right," I said.

"I love pecan pie. You've got a deal."

"How many people will there be?"

"About seven, including us."

"How many pies?"

"I usually bring four. An apple, cherry, pumpkin, and mincemeat."

"Does anyone still eat mincemeat?"

"Grandma Hitesman does. She's ninety-six. When she dies, the industry will crumble."

I laughed. "Maybe you could pick that one up."

"I could do that."

We both looked back down at the calendar.

"The next week is our firm's Christmas party," Nicholas said. "Saturday, December first."

"The one at La Caille?" I asked.

He nodded.

"That's the week of my work party too," I said. "It's that Wednesday."

"Can you do both?"

"Absolutely. But I should warn you, it's not going to be La Caille. It's not even going to be Burger King, for that matter."

"I don't care," he said.

"You have no idea how nice it will be to go with someone this year. Ever since I divorced, I've been the odd one out."

"I think I have an idea," he said. "That's why we're doing this."

The next week there were two days marked

on the calendar. December sixth and seventh. "What are these?"

His expression fell. "It's nothing," he said in a way that made me sure that it was. "It's just . . . something I do." He quickly moved on. "The next week, on the fourteenth, is the partners' party. Then the week after that I have to fly to New York City to meet with one of our clients, so we won't get together that week." He looked up at me. "Unless you come to New York with me."

I couldn't tell if he was serious. "I'm afraid that would be out of my budget."

"Travel expenses are in the contract."

I looked at him. "You're serious." To tell the truth, the idea of going to New York at Christmas thrilled me. "Let's see how things go."

"That's wise," he replied.

"Then there's nothing until Christmas Eve?"

"What are your plans for Christmas Eve?" he asked.

I was embarrassed to tell him that I hadn't anything planned. "Nothing. Yet."

"How about we have dinner?"

"That would be nice. Where?"

"I don't know, we can decide that later. We have seven weeks."

"And then we're done," I said.

He slowly nodded. "Exactly. The agreement is fulfilled, the contract is terminated." He slid his calendar into his briefcase, then stood. "I better get back. I'll see you tomorrow at lunch, then tomorrow evening for the play."

"Thank you for lunch," I said. I held up the calendar. "And for all this."

"It's my pleasure. I'm looking forward to it."

"Me too."

He looked into my eyes and said, "Elise."

"Yes?"

"No more complaints about gifts. It's been a long time since I've had anyone to give to, and I'm having a lot of fun. Don't ruin it for me. Okay?"

I nodded and smiled. "If you insist."

His serious expression gave way to a smile. "I insist. Have a good day."

As he started to go I said, "Nicholas."

He turned back. "Yes?"

"What kind of car do you drive?"

He looked puzzled. "Why?"

"Zoey wanted to know."

He grinned mischievously. "Tell her it's a very expensive one." He blew me a kiss and walked off. As he disappeared from sight, I took out my scarf and put it around my neck. It had been a long time since I had felt that warm.

# Chapter Seven

*Why is it that we so easily confide secrets
to strangers that we so carefully hide
from ourselves?*

## ELISE DUTTON'S DIARY

I once read that the secret to happiness is having
something to do, something to look forward to,
and someone to love. It must be true even if the
love is contractual. The next morning was the
first time in a long time that I woke happy. I
followed my usual routine of shower, hair, health
shake, then, looking at myself in the mirror, I
took extra time for my makeup. I used to be
good at makeup, but that was before I stopped
caring. You don't take care of things you don't
value.

I was a few minutes late to work, but,
considering all the late evenings and unpaid over-
time I'd pulled over the years, I wasn't worried.

"You're late," Zoey said as I walked into the
office. She was applying mascara.

"I know," I said simply.

Around ten o'clock we were having staff meeting when the bell on our door rang. "I'll get it," Zoey said, standing. She was always the first to offer. She hated meetings.

Five minutes later, when Zoey hadn't returned, Mark said, "Elise, would you please remind Zoey that we're in the middle of a staff meeting?"

"Sure," I said. I walked out into the front lobby. Zoey was just standing there in a room filled with flowers. "The man's smitten," she said, shaking her head in disbelief. "It took two deliverymen to bring them all in."

There were twelve dozen roses, half white, half red. If Nicholas was making a point about sending me whatever he wanted, he'd succeeded. A minute later Cathy walked out. "Holy florist. We're going to have to start charging this guy rent." She looked at me. "What are you going to do with all those?"

"I have no idea," I said.

"The delivery people said they'd be back to take them to your apartment," Zoey said. "Here's the card that came with them."

I unsealed the envelope.

*Day 4. Next time you complain that I'm spending too much I'm doubling it. Looking forward to tonight.*
*—Nicholas*

I smiled.

"What did he say?" Zoey asked.

"He's looking forward to our date tonight."

"Where are you going?"

"We're going to watch a play. *A Christmas Carol.*"

"That sounds . . . fun." I knew that a play wouldn't be her idea of a good time. She looked at me for a moment, then said, "You know what the problem with all this is?"

I looked at her. "No. What?"

"No one can keep this up forever. Someday it's going to stop. And then it's going to suck."

"It's most certainly going to stop," I said. "The trick is to enjoy the ride while it lasts."

Zoey looked at me with surprise. "When did you get this attitude?" Then she looked closer at me. "Are you wearing eyeliner?"

When I arrived in the food court, Nicholas was already there, sitting at our usual table. He must have been early; he had already bought our food. He smiled when he saw me. "I took the liberty of ordering the usual."

"Thank you," I said, sitting down. I took a bite of my salad. He wore a funny expression, and I guessed that he was waiting for me to comment on the flowers. I decided to play dumb.

Finally he said, "So did you get anything today?"

I looked at him blankly. "Anything? Like what?"

"A special delivery?"

"Hmm, I said. "A special delivery. Oh, you mean like a hundred and forty-four roses?"

He grinned. "That wasn't too *excessive,* was it?"

"No. Just right. And once the delivery people return to get them, my apartment will look like a funeral parlor."

He laughed. "We're still on for tonight?"

"Yes."

"The play starts at seven, so I'll pick you up around six-thirty?"

"Okay," I said.

"Then, if you're not too tired, we'll get some dinner after."

"Sounds nice."

"Anything in particular?"

"No. Surprise me." Just going out to dinner was surprise enough.

It was snowing when I got home from work. As usual, my apartment was a mess, so I picked up the place or, at least, organized the chaos—throwing my clothes in a hamper and loading the dishwasher. I was about to freshen up for the play when the doorbell rang. *He better not be early,* I thought. He wasn't. It was the florist. "I've got your flowers," the man said.

I looked around my tiny apartment. "Bring them in."

"Where do you want them?"

"Wherever they'll fit," I replied.

My apartment was on the second floor of the building, and it took the man fifteen minutes to bring all the roses in from his truck. By the time he finished, it was twenty-five after. I quickly changed into some more comfortable jeans and a sweater, brushed back my hair, then went to put on some perfume but couldn't find any. *Girl, you've got to get back with it.*

I remembered that I had an unopened bottle of perfume in the bottom of my closet—a gift from the girls at the office for my birthday last spring. I tore open the package and was spraying it on when the doorbell rang. I looked at myself one more time in the mirror, then hurried out past the garden of flowers, grabbing my coat on the way.

I opened the door. Nicholas was standing there holding a bouquet of yellow gerbera daisies. I almost laughed when I saw them. "You're kidding, right?"

"I wasn't sure what else to bring you," he said.

"Let me find something to put these in. Come on in."

He laughed when he saw the flowers splayed out over my front room. "You almost need a machete to get through here."

"Almost," I said.

I couldn't find a vase (other than the ones in my front room), so I filled a pitcher with water and arranged the flowers in it. When I came back out Nicholas was examining a picture on my wall of me with my sister.

"Is this your sister?" he asked.

"Yes."

"What's her name?"

"Cosette."

"As in *Les Misérables*?"

"Yes. My father liked the book. Shall we go?"

"Sure," he said. Then added, "You look nice."

"Thank you. So do you." He was dressed casually in a dark green knit sweater that was a little wet on the shoulders from falling snow. "I don't think I've ever seen you out of a suit."

"It's rare, but I do dress down on occasion."

I took his hand as we walked down the stairs. His car was parked out front, a white BMW sedan. He held the door open for me as I got in. The interior was immaculate and smelled like cinnamon. The seats and doors were two-toned leather, embossed like a football. He shut the door, then went around and climbed in.

"You have a nice car."

"Thank you. I just got it a few months ago. The dealer said it's good in snow. I hope he's right. I turned your seat warmer on. If it's too hot you can adjust it."

"Thanks."

He started the car. The heater and the windshield wipers came on simultaneously, along with a

Michael Bublé Christmas album. "Is this music okay?"

"I love Bublé," I said.

"Then Bublé you will have."

"It smells good in here," I said.

"*You* smell good. What is it? Lovely?"

"How in the world did you know that?"

"My paralegal wears it." He pulled a U-turn, then drove out of my complex. "Thanks again for going to this with me. I've wanted to do this for a while."

"It's my pleasure," I said. "I told Cathy where we were going, and she said she loves it. Her family goes every year."

"Who's Cathy?"

"Sorry, she's our bookkeeper."

"Are all of your friends from work?"

I frowned, embarrassed by the question. "Yes."

He glanced over. "It happens. All my friends are lawyers. Except you."

Something about how he had said that made me glad. "Tell me about this play," I said.

"Hale Centre Theatre. They've been doing this for a long time. I'm kind of a sap when it comes to Christmas. I watch *A Christmas Carol* on TV at least twice every holiday season. My favorite television version is the one with George C. Scott."

"Me too," I said. "I mean, that's my favorite version too."

The Hale Centre Theatre was located on the

west side of the valley, about fifteen minutes from my apartment. The place was crowded. We picked up our tickets at Will Call, then Nicholas asked, "Would you like a drink or a snack?"

I glanced over at the concession stand. "Maybe some popcorn."

"Okay. Wait, it's not popcorn, it's kettle corn."

"What's the difference?"

"You'll like it," he said. "It has sugar."

"How do you know I like sugar?"

"You eat it on your salad," he said.

We got a small box of kettle corn and climbed the stairs to the theater's entrance. The theater was in the round, and, not surprisingly, we had good seats, though in a theater that small I'm not sure there were any bad ones.

After we had sat down I ate some kettle corn and said, "Picking up our tickets at Will Call reminded me of something dumb I did."

"Tell me."

"When I first started at ICE, Mark, he's the owner, sent me over to Modern Display to pick up some plastic display holders for a convention we were doing. He said to get them from Will Call. When I got there I went up to the sales counter and asked for Mr. Call. There were two men there, and they both looked at me with funny expressions. One asked the other, 'Do you know a Call here?' He said, 'No.' Then he said to me, 'I'm sorry, there's no Mr. Call here. Do you know his first name?' I said, 'I think it's William or Will. My boss just said to pick it up from Will Call.' They laughed for about five minutes before someone told me why."

Nicholas laughed. "I did that exact same thing once."

"Really?"

"No, I'm not that dumb."

I threw a piece of kettle corn at him.

"So here's some trivia for you," he said. "Did you know that the original name that Dickens gave his book was much longer? Its real title is *A Christmas Carol in Prose: Being a Ghost Story of Christmas*. A carol is a song or a hymn, so the abbreviated title doesn't really make sense."

"I've never thought of that," I said.

"It's a much more influential book than most people realize. In a way, Dickens invented Christmas."

"I'm pretty sure Christmas existed before Dickens was born."

"True, but before *A Christmas Carol*, Easter was the biggest Christian celebration. December twenty-fifth was no more consequential than Memorial Day. In fact, the colony of Massachusetts had a law on the books prohibiting the celebration of the holiday. Christmas was considered a pagan celebration, and observing Christmas might cost you a night in the stocks."

"Why is that?"

"Mostly the timing, I suspect. The reason we celebrate Christmas on the twenty-fifth has nothing to do with Christ's birth. In fact, we have no idea when Christ was born. The twenty-fifth was designated as Jesus's birthday by Pope Julius I, in order to attract new Roman members to the church because they were already celebrating the day in honor of the pagan god of agriculture. Which is why Christmas not so coincidentally takes place near the winter solstice."

"I had no idea," I said.

"Also interesting is that historically, Dickens and Friedrich Engels were contemporaries. They were both in Manchester, England, at the same time and they were equally repulsed by the workers' living conditions."

"Who is Friedrich Engels?"

"He was Karl Marx's inspiration for the *Communist Manifesto*. The early nineteenth century was a dark time for the workingman. The majority of the children born to working-class parents died before the age of five. So while Engels wrote about a political revolution, Dickens was writing about a different kind of revolution—a revolution of the heart. He was writing about the things he wrote about in his other books, the welfare of children and the need for social charity."

"How do you know all this?"

"I'm a lawyer," he said, which again made no sense to me.

"What does that have to do with—"

"Shh," he said, laying his finger across his lips. "The play is starting."

As the lights came up at the end of the first half, just before Scrooge meets the Ghost of Christmas Yet to Come, I excused myself to go to the ladies' room. When I returned Nicholas was standing near our seats, talking to a beautiful young woman. She looked to be in her late twenties, with big brown eyes and coffee brown hair that fell past her shoulders.

"Elise, this is Ashley," Nicholas said. "We used to work together."

She smiled at me. "I was Nick's legal secretary. It's nice to meet you."

"It's nice to meet you," I echoed. I took Nicholas's hand, which she noticed.

"Where's Hazel tonight?" Nicholas asked.

"With Grandma," she said. "Kory and I needed a night out. Looks like you did too." She turned to me. "Nick's the best boss I've ever had, but an insatiable workaholic. I'm glad to see someone got him out of the office for a change."

"This is the first time I've seen him without a tie," I said.

"I can believe that. I'm pretty sure that he sleeps with one on." She turned back to Nicholas. "It's good to see you. You take care." She leaned forward, and they hugged. Then she walked around to a section directly across the theater from ours.

"How long did she work for you?" I asked.

"Three, almost four years. A year ago she quit to have a baby."

"She likes you."

"We worked well together," he said simply.

We sat back in our seats as the lights dimmed and the second half began. Near the end of the performance I heard a sniffle. I furtively glanced over at Nicholas as he wiped his eyes with a crumpled Kleenex.

After the show the cast came out to the lobby to shake hands with the audience. We thanked them for the performance before walking out into the cold night air.

"That was really good," I said.

"I'm glad I finally got to see it."

"It affected you."

He nodded. "It's about redemption and hope." He looked me in the eyes. "Hope that we can be better than our mistakes."

His words struck me to the core. It was as if he knew me intimately. It took me a moment to respond. "Thank you for taking me."

"You're welcome," he said. When we got back to his car he asked, "Are you hungry?"

"Famished."

"Do you like Thai food?"

"I've never had it. But I'd like to try it."

"Good. I know a place."

The restaurant was less than ten minutes from

the theater. A young Thai woman seated us in a vacant corner of the restaurant and handed us menus. I looked mine over. "I have no idea what to order."

"How about I order a few dishes and we'll share?"

I set down my menu. "Perfect."

When our waitress came, Nicholas ordered a bunch of things I couldn't even pronounce, then said, "You'll love it." Then added, "Maybe."

A few minutes later the waitress set two bowls of white soup on the table in front of us. "What's this?" I asked.

"Coconut milk soup."

Our waitress returned with a large bowl of noodles, two platters of curry dishes, and a large bowl of sticky rice.

I dished up my plate with a little of everything. I liked it all, which wasn't too surprising, since everything was sweet.

In the middle of our dinner Nicholas asked, "Have you lived in Salt Lake your whole life?"

"No. I was born in Arizona. I lived there until I was fourteen."

"Where in Arizona?"

"Chino Valley. Near Prescott. Do you know Arizona?"

"A little," he replied. "I've spent some time there. What brought you to Utah?"

"My father."

"Work?"

"No. It's more complicated than that."

"How so?"

I hesitated. "My father was an interesting man."

"By *interesting* do you mean, a 'fascinating individual' or a 'living hell'?"

I laughed. "More of the latter," I said. Nicholas continued looking at me in anticipation. "Are you sure you really want to hear this?"

"I love to hear people's histories," he said. "*Especially* the interesting ones."

"All right," I said. "My father was fanatical. Actually, that's putting it mildly. He thought the world was going to hell, and since the 'lunatic' Californians were buying up all the land around us, he sold our farm and moved us to a little town in Utah of ninety-six people. We made it an even hundred."

"What town?"

"You've never heard of it."

"Try me."

"Montezuma Creek."

"You're right," he said. "Why there?"

"Because it was about as far from civilization as you could get. And, don't laugh, because there was only one road into town and he could blow it up when the Russians invaded."

"Really?"

"It's true," I said. "He had a whole shed of dynamite and black powder." I shook my head.

"The biggest thing that ever happened in Montezuma Creek was when the Harlem Globetrotters came through town. I don't know what brought them to such a small town. I guess they weren't that big anymore, but the whole town showed up. I think the whole county showed up."

"What did your father do in Montezuma Creek? To provide?"

"We had greenhouses. Big ones. We mostly grew tomatoes. We sold them to Safeway."

"How did you end up in Salt Lake?"

"I just got out as fast as I could."

"Didn't like the small-town life?"

"I didn't like my father," I said softly. "He talked constantly about the end of days and the world being evil and corrupt, but the truth is, *he* was evil and corrupt. And violent and cruel. I lived in constant fear of him. I remember I was at our town's little grocery store when a man I'd never met said to me, 'I feel sorry for you.' When I asked why, he said, 'That you have that father. He is one awful man.'

"My father was always trying to prove that he was in control. Once I told him I was excited because we were going to have a dance lesson at school, so he made me stay home that day for no reason. Some days he would keep us home from school just to prove that the government couldn't tell him what to do.

"He would rant that the police were just the henchmen of an Orwellian government conspiracy, and anytime one tried to pull him over, he'd try to outrun them. It was a perverse game with him. Sometimes he'd get away, sometimes they'd catch him, and they'd drag him out of the car and handcuff him, which only proved his point that the police were brutal. He lost his license, but that was irrelevant to him. He didn't see that the government had any right to tell a person whether they could drive or not.

"I remember watching him being handcuffed and arrested, and I was afraid they were going to take me to jail too. I grew up terrified of police. Police and snakes."

"Snakes?" Nicholas said.

I nodded. "My father used to think it was funny to chase me around the house with live rattlesnakes. I remember him holding one on a stick and it trying to strike at me." I looked down. "I have a terrible phobia of snakes. I can't even see a picture of one without being paralyzed with fear."

"That's abuse," Nicholas said.

I nodded. "He was all about abuse. Only he didn't see it that way. He saw us as property, and, if something is yours, you can do what you want to it. Property doesn't have needs. Property only exists to suit *your* needs.

"One time we had a problem with our truck. He

said it was the carburetor, so he made my sister lie on the engine under the hood and pour gasoline into the carburetor while we drove. What kind of father puts his kid under the hood of a moving vehicle?"

"A deranged one," Nicholas said. "What were his parents like?"

"That's the strange part. My grandparents were sweet people. They used to apologize to me about him. Once my grandmother said, 'We don't know what happened to him, dear.'

"He considered reading for entertainment a waste of time. Once he found me in my room reading a Mary Higgins Clark book and he was furious. He called me lazy and said that if I had time to waste, he'd find something for me to do. He made me go out and move the entire wood-pile from one side of the house to the other. It took me four hours. And I was terrified the whole time, because snakes hid in the woodpile. Twice I found rattlesnakes when bringing in firewood."

Nicholas looked sad. "I'm so sorry."

"Thanks," I said. "More than anything, I just wanted to be loved. In a small town like that, there aren't a lot of romantic options. Once I told my father that a boy walked me home from school, and my father beat me and sent me to my room for the night. He called me a tramp. I believed him. I felt so guilty about it."

"You couldn't see that you'd done nothing wrong?"

I shook my head. "The thing is, <u>when you grow up with crazy, you don't know what sane is.</u> You might suspect that there's something better, but until you see reality, it's impossible to comprehend.

"A year after I was married I caught my father with another woman. They were kissing. He lied about it at first, but when he saw that I didn't believe him, he admitted that he was having an affair and told me not to tell my mother."

"Did you?"

"No. But not because he said not to. My mother was kind of a doormat. It would have done nothing but humiliate her. She found out later on her own. It's the only time I ever saw her yell at him. But she still didn't leave him. He had alienated all of her family, so she really had no place to go.

"By the time I turned eighteen I couldn't take it anymore. I left high school and got a job more than three hundred miles away, at Bryce Canyon Lodge as a waitress. It was a good gig. They paid almost nothing, a dollar six an hour, but there was free food and lodging, and we got to keep all our tips. We just had to work two meals a day. The people at the lodge were really nice, and I made a lot of money in tips. Enough to pay for my first year of college.

"Every now and then celebrities would come through. I met Robert Redford once. He was really nice. He told me that I smelled like lilacs. I met people from all over. That's when I knew that I wanted to travel and see the world. But I think it was probably more that I wanted to get as far away from Montezuma Creek as I could. I wanted to get as far away from my father as I could." I forced a smile. "I didn't get too far, I guess. I carried a lot of it with me."

"It's hard to leave some things behind," Nicholas said. "So how did you turn out so lovely?"

I just looked at him. Suddenly my eyes welled up with tears. He reached over and took my hand. When I could speak I said, "Thank you."

"Is your father still alive?"

"No. He died of cancer. Both of my parents did. They both grew up near the Nevada Proving Ground, where the government tested nuclear weapons. For dates they used to go out and watch them detonate atom bombs. Crazy, huh? They didn't know better."

Nicholas just shook his head. "He was a downwinder."

"You're familiar with that?"

"Intimately. Our firm handled a massive lawsuit against the federal government involving downwinders."

"Well, I'm sure my father was part of it." I sighed. "I remember going back and seeing him before he died. He was so frail and weak. I thought, *Is this really the man who filled me with such terror, who towered over my past?* He was nothing. His meanness drained out. He was like a snake without venom. He was nothing but a hollow shell."

Nicholas looked at me, then said, "They that see thee shall narrowly look upon thee, and consider thee, saying, Is this the man that made the earth to tremble, that did shake kingdoms? Isaiah 14:16."

"You read the Bible," I said.

"At times," he replied. "So you went to college in Salt Lake?"

"No. I went to Snow College. My best friend from Montezuma Creek asked if I wanted to be her roommate, so I took her up on it."

"Snow College," he said. "Isn't that in Manti?"

"It's the town next to it," I said. "Ephraim. The one with all the turkey farms. Sometimes turkey dander would settle over the school. I was horribly allergic to it."

"To turkey dander?" he asked.

I nodded. "That's where I met my ex-husband, Dan." I paused. "Dan. Dan-der. I never made that connection before."

Nicholas laughed. "Dander. I like that."

"Dan was from Salt Lake. He was doing his general ed at Snow because it was cheaper than the University of Utah. He was ambitious back then. He promised to show me the world. Then

71

he left college to sell water purifiers. Dan wasn't very nice, but that's what I was used to. The truth was, he was my way out. A counselor once told me that Dan was my 'vehicle of emancipation.' I think she was right. I followed Dan to Salt Lake, and we got married. We were married for eight years before he divorced me."

"Why did he divorce you?"

I looked at Nicholas and said, "Wasn't there a clause in our contract about deep and probing questions?"

"You're right. I crossed the line."

"Well, technically, we crossed the line about ten minutes ago," I said. "It's okay. Dan divorced me because he was cheating on me with my best friend."

"Your college roommate?"

"Yes. He's now married to her."

"Remarkable," Nicholas said. "What was your divorce settlement like?"

"Not good. It's not like Dan had much money, but I didn't get anything."

"Sounds like you had a poor attorney."

"No, he had a poor client."

"Why?"

I looked down. "Some people are born thinking they're pretty important. Some aren't."

Nicholas nodded slowly as if he understood.

I took a deep breath. "So now that I've spilled all my secrets, let's talk about you."

"That's a nonstarter," he said.

"Really? After I just shared my entire life history, you're holding out on me?"

"I'm only saving you from boredom."

"I think there are some answers that might interest me."

"Such as?"

"To begin with, why aren't you married?"

He looked at me for a moment, then said, "Isn't that why I asked for this contract? So I didn't have to answer that question?"

"I still want to know."

He looked at me thoughtfully and after a moment said, "A lot of people aren't married. A lot of people are married who shouldn't be."

"You're evading the question."

"It's complicated," he said.

"Is that all I get?"

"For now," he said.

"Then tell me about your childhood."

He frowned. "It's nowhere near as exciting as yours. I was born and raised in the Sugar House area. My parents were quiet, conservative Mormons. I went to church until I was sixteen, until . . ." He stopped and a shadow fell over his face. "Until things changed."

"What happened?"

"Just things," he said. "My dark ages. It took me a few years, but I pulled myself out. From then on it was all school and work. I finished college and took the LSAT. I got accepted to Stanford Law School on a scholarship, graduated at the top of my class, then came back to Utah to practice law."

"You started working at the firm you're at now?"

He hesitated before answering. "No, I worked at the prosecutor's office. I kept beating them in court, so they made me an offer."

"That must be nice," I said.

"What must be nice?"

"To be wanted like that."

He suddenly went quiet. Then he said, "I'm sorry. That whole conversation got pretty heavy. I just wanted to get to know you better."

"Well, you know it all now."

"Do I?"

I didn't answer. After a moment of silence he picked up the check. "Let's get you home."

It was cold in the restaurant's parking lot, and our breath froze in front of us. The cars were all covered with a thin veneer of freshly fallen snow. He started his car, turned on the heater and window defroster, then got out and scraped the windows. When he got back in, his hands were wet and red with the cold. He rubbed them together.

"Let me see them," I said.

He looked at me curiously, then held them out. I cupped them in my hands and breathed on them.

He smiled. "Thank you."

We didn't say much on the way home. I suppose I felt talked out. But the silence wasn't uncomfortable. When we pulled up in front of my apartment he said, "Thanks again for going with me."

"It was fun," I replied. "I'm sorry I talked so much."

"I enjoyed learning about you."

"Well, I kind of threw up on you. I guess it's been a while since I've had anyone ask me about myself."

"I'm glad it was me," he said.

I smiled at him, then said, "Me too. Have a good weekend."

"You too. I'll see you Monday."

I got out of the car and walked up the snow-covered sidewalk to my apartment stairs, leaving footprints as I went. Nicholas waited until I reached the door. I turned back and waved. He waved back then drove away.

Not surprisingly, my apartment smelled like roses. I went into my bedroom and undressed, turned out the light, then lay back on my bed.

"Who are you, Nicholas?" I said into the darkness. "And what are you doing with me?"

# Chapter Eight

*People talk of life's storms as if they
are universal experiences. But they're
not. Some people hear thunder while
others touch lightning.*

## ELISE DUTTON'S DIARY

*THREE YEARS EARLIER*

I couldn't sleep because of the pain. At first I
thought it was an upset stomach. Then, as the pain
increased, an ulcer. An ulcer made sense. I was a
worrier. I'd worried my whole life.

While my husband, Dan, slept, I downed a
bottle of Pepto-Bismol, which did nothing to
relieve my agony. Finally, at four in the morning,
I woke Dan, and he reluctantly drove me to
St. Mark's Hospital emergency room. It wasn't
an ulcer, it was appendicitis. And my appendix
had burst. I was rushed into surgery and spent
the next two days in intensive care being fed
massive doses of antibiotics to attack the infec-

tion that had set in. On the third day I had shown enough progress that they moved me out of the ICU.

Dan came to see me that afternoon bearing a bouquet of spring flowers. It was only the second time I had seen him since I was admitted, and, in spite of his absence, I was glad to see him. We had talked for only about a half hour when he said he had to get back to work. Dan was working as a telemarketer and managed a phone solicitation office. After he left I was just lying there looking at the flowers when one of my nurses walked in. Keti was a Tongan woman as wide as she was tall.

"Oh, aren't you lucky," she said. "Somebody loves you."

I smiled. "Aren't they beautiful? They're from my husband."

"You hang on to him, honey. I can't tell you the last time my husband brought me flowers." She looked up at me. "Oh wait, I don't have a husband." She walked to my side. "How are you feeling?"

"It hurts where they made the incision."

"That's usual. An appendectomy is like a cesarean, except you don't get a baby for it."

"I feel a little warm."

"Warm? Like a fever?"

"Yes."

She sidled up to my bed. "I was just about to

check your temperature." She rubbed an electronic thermometer across my forehead and frowned. "You have a temperature. A hundred and two point four. I don't like that."

"What does that mean?"

"Maybe a little infection." She checked my chart. "You're already on a pretty high dosage of antibiotics, but let me see if the doctor wants to up your dose a little."

"Thank you."

As she scribbled on her clipboard, I heard the vibration of a cell phone. We both looked around to see where it was coming from, then Keti discovered an iPhone lying next to the flowers. "Is this yours?"

"No. It's probably my husband's. He must have left it." I reached out my hand for it. "I'll text his office and let them know I have it."

"How sweet," Keti said looking at the screen. "Amore. Is that what he calls you?"

"Amore?" I looked at her blankly. "No . . ."

She handed me the phone. "It's right here."

### Amore Mia
Text Message

*Amore? My love?* Who's calling my husband Amore? No, that's not how it works. Who is my husband calling Amore Mia? I pressed the notification.

### Amore Mia
Are you on your way?
October 11, 2009 1:04 PM

I started reading backward throh the thread of messages.

### Amore Mia
Your so good
October 11, 2009 12:55 PM

### Dan the Man
Not now. After she is back home.
Feeling better
October 11, 2009 12:54 PM

### Amore Mia
:( When are you going to tell her?
October 11, 2009 12:52 PM

### Dan the Man
She's doing okay. Made it
through the hard time
October 11, 2009 12:51 PM

### Amore Mia
After. Pretty please? You'll be glad! ;-)
How is Elise?
October 11, 2009 12:49 PM

### Dan the Man
:) On way to hospital to see Elise. I love you
October 11, 2009 12:45 PM

**Amore Mia**
Just had the sweetest dream of you.
I miss you. Can you come over?
October 11, 2009 12:42 PM

**Amore Mia**
Ditto. Ditto. Ditto. Please. Please.
Please!!!!!!!!!!!!!!!!!!!!!!!!!
October 11, 2009 10:07 AM

**Dan the Man**
Floating. Last night was unbelievable.
We need a rerun ASAP!!!!!!!!!!!!!!
October 11, 2009 9:42 AM

**Amore Mia**
How is my dreamboy today?
October 11, 2009 9:39 AM

There were more. Many more. I couldn't read them because my eyes were filled with tears.

"Honey?" Keti said.

I looked up at her. "My husband is cheating on me."

"I'm sorry."

Just then Dan walked back into the room. "Hi, babe, I forgot my phone."

I looked at him, shaking, unable to speak.

"Why are you crying?" He looked at Keti. "Is she in pain?"

"I would think so," Keti said, her eyes narrow with anger.

"Can you get her something for it?"

"Not for this pain."

He looked at her quizzically, then back over at me. "Honey . . ."

"Who is she?" I said.

"I'll check on your antibiotic," Keti said, making her way toward the door. It sounded ridiculous, like telling someone in a hurricane that you would be back to wash their windows. She brushed by Dan on the way out.

"Who?" he asked, his eyes stupidly wide.

"Who is Amore Mia?"

He stepped toward me. "I don't know what you're talking about."

I held up his phone. "Who is Amore Mia?"

"Elise . . ."

"If you have something to tell me, tell me now."

"It's nothing. She's nothing."

"I read the texts. Don't lie to me."

For a moment we looked at each other, then he breathed out slowly, as if he'd resigned himself. "Okay, so you caught me. I'm having an affair."

"Who is she?"

He looked even more uncomfortable.

"Do I know her?"

"Kayla," he said.

The only Kayla I knew was my best, and only, friend and the thought that she would cheat with my husband was so far beyond possibility that I couldn't process it. "Kayla who?"

"Kayla," he said again but with more emphasis.

*"My Kayla?"*

"Yeah."

My pain doubled. When I could speak I asked, "How long has this been going on?"

"I don't know."

"How long?"

"A while."

I broke down crying again. He stepped forward and put his hand on my arm. "Elise."

I pulled away. "Don't touch me."

"Elise," he said in the condescending register he used when he thought I was being overly dramatic.

"Go away," I said. "Go to your . . . *amore.*"

"I'm not leaving," he said.

"Get out of here!" I shouted.

Just then Keti walked back into the room. She must have heard our conversation because she looked angry. "You need to leave," she said, pointing a sausage finger at Dan.

"She's my wife," Dan said. "I don't need to go anywhere."

Her voice rose. "She's *my* patient and this is *my* house, and if she wants you to leave, you leave." She walked to a button on the wall. "Or should I call security?"

He glared at her, then looked back at me. "It's

your fault, Elise. You're the one who ruined our lives. You have no one to blame but yourself." He turned and walked away. Two days later I was still in the hospital when Dan filed for divorce.

# Chapter Nine

*Today I overheard Zoey and Cathy
talking about Nicholas. It's not what
they said about him that hurts. It's what
they were implying about me.*

## Elise Dutton's Diary

Mondays were always the hardest days at ICE. Invariably there would be some crisis that had occurred over the weekend: lost luggage, a canceled flight, a broken-down bus, or any of the thousand things that can go wrong when traveling with groups. That doesn't even include the things our students did. Like the time three of the boys were arrested in New York for dumping soda on people on the sidewalk below the hotel.

This Monday was no different. It began with our usual staff meeting and Mark ranting about a phone call he'd received over the weekend from a parent whose daughter claimed she had gotten pregnant on one of our trips. The mother had concluded that it was all our fault. I had to contact the teacher who had chaperoned the excursion and tell her what had happened. She already knew. The mother had already gone after her as well, threatening her with a lawsuit and assorted calumny.

I had just hung up the phone with the teacher when Zoey brought in a package and set it on my desk. All she said was "Here."

Happy for the distraction, I unwrapped the paper, then opened the box. Inside was a beautiful, ornate hand mirror. It was oval-shaped with a twisted handle. The frame was tarnished silver that looked almost pewter. I opened the note.

*Elise, Happy Day 7*
*Thank you for an enlightening weekend. I've sent you a new mirror. Hopefully it works better than the one you've been using.*
*—Nick*

*P.S. This is an 1807 antique. The metal is silver. The woman at the antique shop said the best way to clean it is with a cup of white vinegar, a Tbsp of baking soda, and a pinch of salt.*

"So what did you get today?" Zoey asked.

I held up the mirror. "A hand mirror. It's an antique."

"It's pretty," she said simply, then left my office.

About a half hour later I went out to use the bathroom and was in one of the stalls when Zoey and Cathy came in together. It was soon obvious that they didn't know I was there.

"So what do you think of all this?" Zoey asked.

"All what?" Cathy replied.

"Elise's sugar daddy."

"Good for her," Cathy said. "She needed something. Have you met the guy?"

"No. But I'm not looking forward to it. You know what they say, the amount of money a guy spends on a woman is in inverse ratio to his looks. He's probably some fat, bald guy with ear hair."

"At least he's rich," Cathy said.

"Rich doesn't make a man hot," Zoey said.

"No, but it can hide a lot of ugly," Cathy said, laughing.

I was furious. I was about to say something I would no doubt regret, but I calmed myself down. I waited until they left before going back to the office. When I got to my desk I looked up Nicholas's law firm's number and dialed. A professional voice answered. "Derr, Nelson and McKay."

"Hi. I'm calling for Nicholas Derr."

"Just a moment please."

The music on hold was Rachmaninoff, which I knew only because I was an Eric Carmen fan. A half minute later a young female voice answered, "Nicholas Derr's office. This is Sabrina speaking. How may I help you?"

"Hi, Sabrina. I'm calling for Nicholas."

"Mr. Derr is in a meeting right now, may I tell him who's calling?"

"It's not important. This is Elise."

There was hardly a pause. "Elise Dutton?"

I was surprised that she knew who I was. "Yes."

"Just a moment, please."

I was on hold for less than ten seconds before Nicholas answered. "Elise."

"Nicholas, I'm sorry to bother you."

"I'm pleased you called, unless you called to cancel lunch, in which case, I'm pleased to hear your voice, but not that you called."

I smiled. "No, I'm not calling to cancel. I just wanted to see if you would do something for me."

"Name it."

"Would you mind coming to my office today to get me for lunch?"

"I would love to."

"I'm in office 322."

"I know."

Of course he did.

"Thank you for the mirror," I said. "It's pretty."

"Like you," he replied. "I'll see you at twelve-thirty. Bye."

I hung up the phone. "Fat and bald with ear hair," I said.

Then I realized what I had done. He was going to meet perfect Zoey.

Nicholas was punctual. I heard Zoey greeting him with her come-hither voice. "Hi. May I help you?"

I waited inside my office, listening to the exchange. "I'm here for Elise," he said.

"May I tell her who's calling?"

"Nicholas," he said.

Long pause. "You're Nicholas?"

"You must be Zoey."

"Yes. I am." I had never heard her sound so awkward.

"It's a pleasure meeting you," he said.

"I've heard a lot about you," Zoey said.

"I'm glad to hear that," he said. "I assumed that I was just one of Elise's many men."

Zoey said nothing as I walked out. Nicholas looked over at me and smiled. He couldn't have dressed better for his appearance. He looked gorgeous in an Armani suit with a crisp white silk shirt and crimson tie. "And there she is," he said. He walked up to me and kissed me on the cheek. "I hope it's okay I came by early."

"It's fine," I said.

"Great. I was hoping you'd have time for me to take you to lunch. The owner of the New Yorker is a friend of mine, and he has a special table waiting for us. If you have time, that is."

Just then Cathy walked out of her office. She

stopped when she saw Nicholas. She didn't have to say what she was thinking. "Hi."

Nicholas stepped forward, offering his hand. "Hi, I'm Nicholas."

"Cathy," she said, sounding unsure of herself. "It's nice to meet you."

"Likewise," he said. He turned back to me. "So the New Yorker is okay?"

"Of course," I said, doing my best to sound magnanimous. "Let me get my coat."

As I returned to my office I heard Nicholas say, "The table I can get with a phone call, but Elise, I have to pray she can fit me in."

I walked back into the room, and he reached out his hand to me. "Come on, gorgeous."

"Bye," I said to Zoey. "I might be a few minutes late."

"Take your time," she said meekly.

As we walked out into the hallway, I just looked at him. He was smiling.

"Thank you," I said.

"Is that what you wanted?"

"That was perfect. Are we really going to the New Yorker for lunch?"

"Of course. I told you I'd broaden your culinary horizons."

The New Yorker was just a few blocks from the mall. The restaurant didn't have a formal dress code, but everyone inside was professionally attired. It was the kind of place where movers and shakers met and business deals were made. Needless to say, I had never been there before.

After the hostess had seated us at a table for two, Nicholas leaned forward. "So tell me what that was all about."

"The girls in the office have been intrigued by the gifts you've been sending. I overheard them talking this morning. Zoey said, and I quote, 'the amount of money a guy spends on a woman is in inverse ratio to his looks. He's probably some fat, bald guy with ear hair.' "

"Did I dispel any of that?"

"I think you left them speechless."

"Good," he said. "Fortunately I plucked my ear hairs this morning."

"That's just wrong." I laughed. "Can I tell you something honest?"

"Of course."

"I didn't want you to meet Zoey."

"Why is that?"

"I was afraid you might want to trade up."

"No disrespect, but that would be like trading champagne for Kool-Aid."

I grinned. "That's *totally* disrespectful."

"Not to you," he said.

"And thank you again for the mirror. It's beautiful. As is the thought behind it."

"Did I impress you with the cleaning tips?"

"I was *very* impressed."

He smiled. "I thought you would be. So are you ready to order?"

"No." I looked through the menu. "What do you recommend?"

"The tomato soup is always good," he said.

"Why don't you just order for me?"

"I'd be happy to. Something to drink?"

"I'd like a glass of wine."

"Okay," he said. He ordered a glass of Chianti for me, a cranberry juice for himself, and our meal. That was the first time I realized that I had never seen him drink. I wondered if he did.

As the waiter walked away I asked, "So what's next on our agenda?"

"It's your call. You were going to come up with something for our weekend."

"I have an idea," I said. "There's something I've always wanted to do."

"Name it," he said.

"Do you sing?"

"In the shower."

I nodded slowly. "That will do."

# Chapter Ten

*The Golden Rule is a two-edged sword.*
*If some of us treated others as we*
*treat ourselves, we would be jailed.*

## ELISE DUTTON'S DIARY

I had always looked forward to Fridays, but now even the weekdays were better. The whole office anticipated Nicholas's daily gifts. The FedEx man delivered my Friday gift around eleven.

"What is it?" Cathy asked as I opened the box.

"It's New York cheesecake. It's really from New York."

Cathy read the label. "S&S cheesecake from New York. Zagat rated number one."

"I'll get some plates," I said.

"Really?" Cathy said. "You're going to share?"

"If I ate that much cheesecake by myself, I would look like our Christmas tree."

"Bless you, child," Cathy said.

Mark walked out of his office. "Did someone say cheesecake?"

"Elise is sharing the cheesecake her friend sent her."

He walked over and looked at the box. "S&S cheesecake," he said. "I've heard of that. It's the best. And pricey. They sell it by the ounce. Like gold."

I cut the cheesecake up with a plastic knife, and work stopped while everyone ate. Mark closed his eyes as he savored a bite. "Incredible," he said. "If you don't marry that guy, I will."

"Your wife might have something to say about that," Cathy said.

"It doesn't matter," Zoey said. "I've got first dibs."

Nicholas and I didn't have lunch that day because he was in court, but that evening he picked me up at my apartment at six.

"How was your day?" I asked, as we walked to his car.

"Good. We won."

"Do you always win?"

"No. But more than I lose." He opened the car door for me then walked around and got in. "How was your day?"

"Good," I said. "The cheesecake was a hit."

"It doesn't get better than S&S."

"How did you know about them?"

"I'm not as provincial as you might think."

"Believe me, I've never thought of you as

provincial. You're the most cosmopolitan person I know."

"Well, I'm definitely not that either. I just love cheesecake, and I discovered S&S from a client who sent me one last Christmas. That's one of the advantages of having rich clients."

The holiday traffic was heavy as we made our way downtown to Abravanel Hall, Salt Lake City's main concert hall and home to the Utah Symphony. The hall was designed by the same acoustical consultant who had designed the Avery Fisher Hall renovation in New York and the Kennedy Center in Washington, D.C. In the gold-leafed lobby was a thirty-foot-tall red blown-glass sculpture designed by renowned glass artist Dale Chihuly.

The event I had chosen for us was a *Messiah* sing-in with the Utah Symphony, which basically meant that we were part of a three-thousand-member choir. To make sure we sounded good, the singing organizers brought in a few ringers, peppering the audience with about a hundred voices from the University of Utah and the Mormon Tabernacle Choir. We were handed paper scores as we walked into the concert hall.

"I thought we were going to hear a choir sing the *Messiah*," Nicholas said to me as we found our seats. "I didn't realize we *were* the choir."

"It's more fun this way," I said. "I asked if you sing."

"I just thought you were curious."

We sounded better than I thought we would. After the concert we drove over to Ruth's Chris Steak House. I had the petite filet while Nicholas ordered the Cowboy Ribeye. He also ordered a tomato and onion salad to share, a seared ahi tuna appetizer (something I'd never had before), and a sweet potato casserole, which I could have eaten for dessert.

"How do you eat like this and stay thin?" I asked.

"Simple," he replied. "I don't always eat like this."

"I think I've gained a few pounds since I signed the contract. You're spoiling me," I said. "I'm not sure all this spoiling is a good thing."

"Why would spoiling you not be a good thing?"

"Because in five weeks our contract is going to expire, and then where am I?"

"I don't know," he replied. "Where are you?"

I shrugged. "Certainly not eating here."

He looked at me for a moment, then said, "Do you know what I like most about you?"

"I have no idea," I said.

"How grateful you are. In a world growing increasingly entitled, you are truly grateful. It makes me want to do more for you."

"You already do too much," I said.

"My point exactly," he replied. "You're a beautiful soul."

"Fortunately for me, you don't really know me."

"No, you told me everything there was to know about you last week."

"Not everything."

He was quiet for a moment, then said, "I probably know you better than you think."

The statement struck me as peculiar. "What do you mean by that?"

He paused for another moment before he said, "I'm just a very good judge of character."

"That may be," I said. "But the thing is, you don't know what you don't know. No one's perfect. Some of us aren't even that good."

Looking at me seriously, he said, "What I do know is that everyone makes mistakes. That's why forgiveness is so important. Unfortunately, so many of us are bad at it." He let his words settle before continuing. "When I worked for the prosecutor's office, one of my first cases was a man who had shot to death a clerk at a convenience store. We had video of the crime, and I thought it was an open-and-shut case. But because of a technicality we lost. As we were leaving the court-house, the man slapped me on the back and said, 'Thank you, Counselor.' I said, 'For what?' And he said 'For screwing up the case. Of course I killed him. But there's nothing you can do now.' "

"He confessed?" I asked.

"Right there on the courthouse steps."

"Why didn't you just go back in and tell the judge?"

"It wouldn't have done any good. It's called double jeopardy. He can't be tried again for the same offense. It's in the Fifth Amendment to the Constitution. 'Nor shall any person be subject for the same offence to be twice put in jeopardy of life or limb.' The concept was of such importance to the founding fathers that they actually made an amendment to the Constitution for it. But that's in a court of law. In our hearts, there's no such thing. People punish others over and over for the same mistake. We do it to ourselves. It's not right, but still we do it."

I felt like he was reading my mind. He watched me silently. "Elise, you're not as bad as you think you are. Remember that."

When I could speak I said, "So the man was never punished."

"Actually, his case turned out a little differently. Unfortunately for him, he couldn't leave well enough alone. He wrote a letter to the prosecutor's office, bragging that he'd gotten away with murder and stating very specific details of his crime. We reopened the case based on new evidence, and he was found guilty."

"Fool," I said.

"Yes, he was." Nicholas changed the subject. "So the Hitesmans are very excited that you will be joining us for Thanksgiving. Do you still want to bake those pies?"

"Yes," I said. "Except the mincemeat."

"I've already ordered it. When will you bake the others?"

"Wednesday night after work."

"Would you like some help?" he asked.

"Making pies?"

"I don't know how much help I'll be, but I'll keep you company."

"I would love your help," I said. "And your company."

"Great. I'll be there. I'll bring dinner."

That night as I lay in bed remembering our date, I had a frightening realization. My feelings for Nicholas were growing bigger than the contract I'd signed. I wondered if he felt the same way. Not that it mattered. In spite of everything Nicholas had said about forgiveness and redemption, I knew there was no chance we could ever be more than friends. Not if he knew the truth about me. Not if he knew what I'd done. Not if he knew my darkness.

# Chapter Eleven

*Oftentimes, the hottest fires of hell
are fueled from within.*

ELISE DUTTON'S DIARY

*FIVE YEARS EARLIER*

June 2007 was hot. The whole world was hot. Greece reported their worst heat wave in history with eleven heat-related deaths, and the entire European power grid nearly collapsed beneath unprecedented demand for air-conditioning.

It was equally hot in the western part of the United States. In Salt Lake City temperatures which normally would have been in the high eighties exceeded a hundred degrees. Our apartment's swamp cooler struggled to keep things tolerable, and the first thing I did on waking was turn it on to full before getting ready for work.

Dan never helped in the mornings. He said it wasn't his "thing," whatever that meant. I resented him for that. In spite of the fact that I worked longer days than he did, I would get up at least an hour before him to get ready, make breakfast, then get our little girl, Hannah, fed and ready for the day. The one thing Dan did that was helpful was drop Hannah off at day care, since it was only three blocks from his office.

However even that had now changed. I had wearied of Dan's constant complaints about the cost of Hannah's day care, so a week earlier I had found another place at nearly half the price. Since it was on my way to work, now I would have to leave even earlier to drop her off. I didn't like the place as much as the day care where we'd been taking her, but since Dan's commissions were always down during the summer, I decided it was at least worth giving it a try. I wasn't used to the new routine, and one day I'd forgotten to drop her off and had had to turn around just a block from my work and take her to the new place.

On this morning, Hannah was unusually quiet as I got her out of bed. "Are you tired, sweetie?" I asked.

"Yes, Mama," she replied.

"I'm sorry you had to get up so early. I made you Mickey Mouse pancakes."

She smiled. I fed both of us at the same time. Dan stumbled out of bed as I was finishing up.

"Pancakes," he said dully. Dan was taciturn by nature, at least with me, and before nine o'clock getting more from him than a string of three words was rare.

"What's wrong with pancakes?" I asked.

"Had them yesterday."

"No. I made crepes yesterday because you said you wanted them."

"Same diff," he said, sitting down at the table.

I shook my head as I carried our plates over to the sink. I filled the sink with soapy water, then looked down at my watch. "I'm going to be late. I need to grab Hannah's bag, will you please put her in her car seat?"

"Can't you? I'm eating."

"Come on," I said.

"Whatever," he said, standing.

I quickly brushed my teeth, grabbed Hannah's bag, and ran out to the car. "See you," I said to Dan.

"Bye," he said, waving behind his back.

I threw Hannah's bag into the backseat of my Toyota. I looked back. She was asleep. "Sorry, sweetie," I said softly.

I had just pulled out of our subdivision when my cell phone rang. I checked the number. It was work.

"Hello."

"Elise, it's Shirlee," my boss said. "We've got a problem."

"With who?"

"The Tremonton group. Did you book the Smithsonian for today?"

"No, they're tomorrow."

"No, we changed it, remember?"

I groaned. "That's right."

"They're standing outside the Smithsonian. They're telling them that our vouchers aren't good."

"Just call the office of direct sales. Natalie will let them in."

"Where's the number?"

"It's in my Rolodex on my desk. Look under Smithsonian."

"Just a minute." There was a long pause. "You don't have Smithsonian here."

"Of course I do."

"I looked through all the *S*'s, Elise. It's not here."

I was puzzled. "I don't know where it would be. It's got to be there."

"Do you have it in your phone?"

"No."

Shirlee groaned. "There's the driver on the other line. He's got to go. He's got another pickup."

"Just tell him to wait a second, I'll be right there."

I sped into the office. I pulled into a parking place and ran inside. I had accidentally filed the Smithsonian card under *N* for Natalie. But that's not the only mistake I made. I left my three-year-old Hannah in the car on the hottest day of the year.

I've heard it said that there's no greater pain than losing a child. But there is. It's being responsible for your child's death. The day it happened to me is indelibly etched into my mind. People have questioned the existence of hell, but I can tell you it's real. I've been there. Seeing my beautiful little girl's lifeless body in the backseat of my car was hell.

I don't know how long it took for the switch to connect, but after work when I got to my car I just looked at her, the sight incomprehensible. Why was Hannah in the car? Why wasn't she moving? Then reality poured in like a river of fire. I pulled her out, screaming at the top of my lungs. A crowd gathered around me. I tried CPR, I tried mouth-to-mouth, I prayed with everything I had for a miracle, for a heartbeat, for a single breath, but she had been gone for hours. The world swirled around me like a tide pool, spinning me out of control. The paramedics arrived. The police arrived. There was talk of heatstroke and core temperatures and hyperthermia. I fell to the ground unable to walk, unable to do anything but scream and babble, to plead for my baby's life.

A police officer tried to get information from me, but it was like I wasn't there. My little girl's body was taken. I screamed as they took her away even though she was already gone. My Hannah. My reason for living, was gone.

A woman came and put her arm around me. I don't know who she was. I never saw her again. I wouldn't recognize her if I did. She said little, but she was there. Like an angel. Somehow I could talk to her. "I want to die," I said.

"I know, honey," she said. "I'm so sorry."

Then she was gone. Had I imagined her?

The press arrived with cameras and video cameras. Dan arrived after them. "What have you done?" he shouted at me. *"What have you done?"* I couldn't answer. I couldn't even speak. I was catatonic.

There were discussions on whether I should be tried for murder or manslaughter. There would be an investigation. It had already begun. People were talking to Dan. To Shirlee. To my co-workers. To people who didn't know me well enough to speak about me. *What kind of person was I? What kind of mother was I?* No one asked me. I could have answered the latter. I was the worst kind. The kind who killed her own child.

They put me in a police car and drove me downtown to the station. I waited alone in a room for more than an hour. It seemed like no one knew what to do with me. A few police officers came in and asked me questions. Inane questions. *Did I know she was in the car? Had I left her in the car on purpose? When did I realize she was in the car?* "Probably when I started screaming hysterically and collapsed," I wanted to say.

Then a man about my age came and talked to me. He wasn't with the police. He wore a suit. His voice was calm. Sympathetic. He asked me questions, and I mostly just blinked at him. He told me that he was from the prosecutor's office or someplace official. He finished with his questions and spoke with the police. There was a discussion on whether or not I should be arrested and finger-printed, but the man intervened. The talk of court and jail scared me, but nothing they could do could match the pain I already felt. Someone asked if I wanted a sedative. I turned it down. I deserved to feel the pain. I deserved to feel every barb, every hurt, then, God willing, to die.

And the barbs came. My Hannah's death set off a firestorm of media. The television covered it, reducing my tragedy to four minutes of entertain-ment followed by a commercial for tires. Both newspapers, the *Deseret News* and *The Salt Lake Tribune*, weighed in. There were columns of letters to the editor about me. Some said I deserved life in prison for what I'd done. Some said I should be locked in a car with the windows rolled up. I agreed with the latter. The cruelest thing said was that I had killed my Hannah on purpose.

Most confusing to me was how deeply people I didn't know hated me. The attacks lasted for months. I don't know why strangers went so far out of their way to hate me. Maybe it made them feel like better people. Or better parents. Maybe it convinced them that they would never do such a thing. Maybe it masked their fears that they were flawed like me.

I noticed stories like mine everywhere. One British lawyer called it forgotten baby syndrome. *It's not a syndrome,* I thought. *It's an accident. A horrible, exquisite accident. A failure of humanity.*

Once a psychiatrist on TV spoke out for me. He said, "Our conscious mind prioritizes things by importance, but our memory does not. If you've ever left your cell phone in your car, you are capable of forgetting your child." He pointed out that this was an epidemic and there were scores of stories like mine. In one state three children died in one day. He said that this was a new phenomenon, that ten years ago it rarely happened because parents kept their babies near them in the front seat. Then airbags came, and our babies were put out of the way, where we couldn't see them.

He explained that there were two main reasons that people left babies in cars: change of routine and distraction. I'd had both. He said, rightly, that no punishment society could give could match what I was already feeling. I don't know how he knew. I guess it's his job to know.

Through it all, Dan's moods were as volatile as the Utah weather. He was supportive and sympathetic, then, sometimes in the same hour, angry and brooding. He was always moody. He was gone a lot. I didn't know where he went. I didn't really care. It was easier being alone. I was fired from my job, not that I could have worked. I stayed in bed most of the time, hiding from the world, wishing that I could hide from myself.

Then, one night, I got sick with appendicitis. If I had known that my appendix had already burst, I might not have gone to the hospital. If I had stayed home for just another hour or two, I could have ended it all. I had been given a way out. I don't know why I didn't take it. Perhaps, in spite of my self-loathing and pain, some part of me still longed to live.

As I lay in bed wracked with fever, I thought about my life. It was then that I had an epiphany. It came to me that one day I might see my sweet little girl again. *What if she asked me what I had done with my life?* I was not honoring her by retreating from the world—from life. At that moment I resolved that things might be different. That *I* might be different. That I might be *better*.

Then my husband divorced me.

# Chapter Twelve

*Even in the darkest of days there are
oases of joy. And there's usually pie.*

## ELISE DUTTON'S DIARY

As a rare gesture of magnanimity, Mark closed
the office two hours early on the Wednesday
before Thanksgiving. On the way home from work
I stopped at the grocery store for pie ingredients.
It had been years since I'd made pies. I unearthed
the old cookbook my mother had written her pie
secrets in; that cookbook was one of the few
possessions I got after my mother's death.

Before settling in to bake I put the Mitch Miller
*Holiday Sing Along* CD on my stereo to set the
mood. The truth was, I was already in a good
mood. It seemed that I always was when I was
about to see Nicholas.

Nicholas arrived at my apartment a little before
six. I had finished making all the crusts, and the
cherry and apple pies were in the oven, along
with a baking sheet spread with pecan halves.

"I got here as soon as I could," he said apologetically. He carried a paper coffee cup in each hand, and a large white plastic bag hung from the crux of his arm. He breathed in. "It smells heavenly." He handed me a cup. "I got you a salted caramel mocha."

"How do you always know what I want?"

"It's easy. I find the sweetest thing on the menu and order it."

"You've pretty much got me figured out," I said.

"It's probably sacrilege, but I brought us Chinese for dinner. I got wonton soup, sweet and sour pork, walnut shrimp, and pot stickers."

"Which will all go nicely with pumpkin pie," I said. We walked into the kitchen. Nicholas set the bag of Chinese down on the table.

"So, I'm making apple, cherry, pumpkin, and pecan," I said. "The apple and cherry are already in the oven. They're just about done."

Nicholas examined the latticework on my apple and cherry pies through the oven window. "Those are works of art," he said. "Where did you learn to make pies?"

"My mother. She was famous for her pies. Well, about as famous as you can get in Montezuma Creek. She won a blue ribbon for her cherry pie at the San Juan County fair. It was the only prize she ever won. She hung it in the living room next to my father's bowling trophies." I opened the oven and took out the pies, setting them on the counter to cool. "I don't have a lot of happy memories from my childhood, but when she made pie, life was good. Everyone was happy. Even my father."

"My mother always made pies at special times," Nicholas said, "like the holidays or special family get-togethers. But my favorite part of pie making was after she was done and she would take the leftover dough, sprinkle it with cinnamon and sugar, then bake it."

"I know, right!" I said, clapping my hands. "Piecrust cookies. They're the best. Which is why I made extra dough."

"You're going to make some tonight?" Nicholas asked.

"Absolutely," I said. "When the pies are done."

"So, what fat do you use for your crust? Butter, shortening, or lard?"

"My mother was old school. She said that lard made the flakiest piecrust. She thought butter was lazy and shortening was a sin. She was religious about it."

"People get a little fanatic about pies," Nicholas said.

"I'm just getting ready to mix the pecan pie filling. Would you mind getting the pecans out of the oven? The mitts are right there."

"On it," he said.

While he brought the baking sheet out of the oven, I mixed the other ingredients.

"Where do you want the pecans?" he asked.

"Go ahead and pour them in here," I said.

"The pecans rise to the top?"

"Like magic."

In the end I made four regular-size pies for Thanksgiving as well as two tart-size pies—one pecan, one pumpkin—for us to eat with our dinner.

After the last of the pies were in the oven, we sat on the floor in the living room and ate our Chinese food with chopsticks. This was followed by the small pies for dessert and piecrust cookies as a postdessert with decaf coffee.

As I finished my coffee I lay back on the carpet. "I'm too full for Thanksgiving dinner."

"No, we're just stretching out our stomachs to get ready for Thanksgiving dinner," Nicholas said.

"That's a brilliant excuse for gluttony," I said.

"My father used to say that," he said. "He used to make a big breakfast Thanksgiving morning."

"I bet your mother loved that."

"Oh yeah, a dirty kitchen to start with."

"Thanks for bringing us dinner," I said. "What was the name of that restaurant?"

"Asian Star," he said. "And it was nothing. If I'd known you were such a good cook, I would have added a clause in the contract requiring you to cook for me."

"You didn't have to," I said. "I'm happy to cook for you whenever you want."

"There's an open-ended commitment," he said.

"Speaking of commitments, how is the contract going?"

"Our contract?"

"The Mistletoe Promise," he said.

I wondered why he was asking. "I think it's going very well."

"So you're glad you signed?"

"Yes."

"Good," he said.

We decided to watch television as we waited for the last of the pies to bake. I turned the lights out, and we sat next to each other on the couch. I handed Nicholas the remote, and he channel-surfed for a few minutes until we came to *It's a Wonderful Life* on PBS.

"Let's watch this," I said. "I love Jimmy Stewart."

"And that Donna Reed," Nicholas said. "That is one low-maintenance woman."

"Like me," I said.

He smiled. "Just like you."

I must have been exhausted, because I don't remember falling asleep next to him. Actually, on him. I woke with my head on his shoulder. I jumped up.

"You're okay," he said.

"The pies?" I said. "I didn't hear the buzzer."

"I got them out. They look perfect. Marie Callender herself would be proud."

He turned off the television, then walked me to my bedroom. I sat down on the edge of the bed, rubbing my forehead and yawning. "Thank you."

"You're welcome. I'll see you tomorrow. I'll just let myself out."

"Nicholas," I said.

"Yes?"

"Are you glad you signed the contract?"

He smiled, then came up next to me and kissed me on the forehead. "I'd do it again."

# Chapter Thirteen

*It seems a long time since I remembered all I have to be grateful for. Perhaps that's why it's been such a long time since I've been really happy.*

## ELISE DUTTON'S DIARY

Thanksgiving arrived with a heavy snowfall, and I woke to the sound of plows scraping the road. Around nine the snow stopped, and the roads were clear by the time Nicholas arrived at two. Traversing a slippery sidewalk, we carried the pies out to his car, laid them on lipped cookie sheets on his backseat, and drove off to Thanksgiving dinner.

"Tell me about the Hitesmans," I said as we drove.

"You'll like them. Good people. Scott is one of those small-town boys who made good." He turned to me. "He grew up in Burley, Idaho, working the potato fields. Went to Yale for law. The firm picked him up out of college."

"What's his wife's name?"

"Sharon. You'll love her. She's one of those people who's always baking bread for the neighbors or visiting people in the hospital."

The Hitesmans lived in a medium-sized home in the northernmost section of the Avenues. A large pine wreath garnished their front door. Nicholas rang the doorbell, then opened the door before anyone could answer. We were engulfed by the warmth of the home, the smell of baking, and the sound of the Carpenters' Christmas music playing from another room.

A woman walked into the foyer to greet us. She looked to be about my age, pretty with short, spiky auburn hair. Over a red knit shirt she wore a black apron that read:

**THE ONLY REASON
I HAVE A KITCHEN
IS BECAUSE IT CAME
WITH THE HOUSE**

"Nicholas," she said joyfully. "And this must be Elise. I'm Sharon."

"Hello," I said. "Happy Thanksgiving."

"Happy Thanksgiving to you too," she returned. She looked down at the pies we carried. "Those look delicious, let me take that from you," she said, taking the cookie sheet from my hands. "Boys, come here. Fast."

Two young boys, close in age, appeared at her side.

"Carry these into the kitchen and don't drop them."

"Okay," they said in unison.

"Now we can properly greet," she said, hugging me first then hugging and kissing Nicholas. "It's so good to see you. You haven't been around much lately."

"Work," he said. "And more work."

"You lawyers work too much. But Scott says your absence might have something to do with your new friend," she said, looking at me. "Elise, we're so pleased you've joined us. Nicholas has told us so much about you."

"Good things, I hope."

"All good," she said. Suddenly her brow fell. "Wait, have we met before?"

"I don't think so."

"You look familiar. I have a pretty good memory for faces. You aren't famous, are you?"

"No."

"You haven't been in the newspaper or on TV?"

I froze. It wasn't the first time someone had asked, but I . . ."

"Sharon," Nicholas said lightly, "stop interrogating her. She just has one of those faces."

Sharon smiled. "She definitely has a pretty one. I'm not often wrong about things like that, but there's always a first."

"Thank you," I said.

"Now come in, come in. We're almost ready to eat. Make yourself at home. I need to check on the rolls, but let me take your coats."

I shrugged off my coat and handed it to her. As she started to turn away, a man, stocky and broad shouldered with blond hair neatly parted to one side, walked up behind her. "St. Nick," he said, extending his hands to Nicholas in greeting.

"Hey, buddy," Nicholas returned. They man-hugged and then, with his arm still across the man's shoulder, Nicholas said to me, "This is Scott."

Scott reached his hand out to me. "So glad you could come. Nick's told us so much about you."

All I could think of was Nicholas's description of Scott as a potato picking Idaho farm boy, which was exactly what he looked like, except without dirt beneath his fingernails. I took his hand. "Thank you. I was glad to be invited."

"I guarantee you won't go away hungry," Scott said. He turned to Nicholas. "I hate to do this today, but can I ask you something about the Avalon case? I've got to get back to them by seven."

"No rest for the wicked," Nicholas said. He turned back to me. "Sorry, I'll be right back. Just . . . mingle."

As they slipped off to Scott's den, I walked into the living room and kitchen area. Adjoining the living room was the dining room, with a long table that was beautifully set with a copper-colored linen tablecloth, gold-trimmed china plates on gold chargers, and crystal stemware. There was a floral centerpiece in autumn colors with two unlit red candles rising from its center.

The two boys were now lying on their stomachs, playing a video game in front of the fireplace. Across from them, on the sofa, was an elderly woman I guessed to be the grandmother. She looked like she was asleep. I drifted toward the kitchen, where Sharon was brushing butter over Parker House rolls.

"May I help?" I asked.

"I could use some help," she said. "Would you mind opening that can of cranberry sauce and putting it on a plate? The can opener is in that drawer right there."

I found the can opener, opened the can, and arranged the sauce.

"Your pies look divine," Sharon said. "Nick usually just picks them up from Marie Callender's."

"Thank you. I like making pies. Except mincemeat. We bought the mincemeat."

"I'm not a mincemeat fan either. It's really just for Grandma."

"That's what Nicholas said."

"He didn't bring it one year. Grandma let him know that she wasn't happy." We both looked over at the old woman. "It's a lot of work making pies. Especially the lattice tops," Sharon remarked.

"I enjoy making them," I said again. "And Nicholas helped."

She looked at me with surprise. "Nicholas helped you make pies?"

"Yes."

"Wow," she said. "You domesticated him. Things must be going well with you two."

I didn't know how to respond. Finally I said, "We're having fun."

"Fun is good. He said you met at work."

"Sort of. We work in the same office building. I'm four floors beneath him."

Sharon donned hot mitts, then opened the oven. "Time to bring out the bird," she said as she pulled a large roaster out and set it on the granite-topped island in the middle of the kitchen. She lifted the lid, exposing a large browned turkey.

At that moment, Nicholas walked in, trailed by Scott. "I see you put her to work," Nicholas said to Sharon.

"I did," Sharon said.

Nicholas said to me, "She comes across as nice, but she's really a heartless taskmaster. Last year she made Scott and me put together the boys' Christmas bikes before we could eat."

"Shhh!" she said. "They're right there. Santa brought those bikes."

Nicholas grinned. "Sorry." He turned to me. "Did you meet Grandma?"

"Not yet," I said. "She's asleep."

"And don't wake her," Sharon said. "Let sleeping dogs lie."

"I heard that," Grandma shouted. "I'm not a dog. I'm old, not deaf."

I glanced furtively at Nicholas, who looked like he might burst out laughing.

"I want a Dr Pepper," she shouted. "No ice."

"Would you mind?" Sharon said to Nicholas. "There's one in the fridge. She likes it in a plastic cup, no ice."

"Sure," he said. He retrieved the soda, poured it into the cup, then took my hand and led me over to the woman. "Here you go, Grandma," he said, offering her the drink.

She snatched it from him, took a long drink, burped, then handed the half full cup back to him without thanks.

"Elise, this is Grandma Wilma," Nicholas said. "Grandma, this is Elise."

"Did you bring the mincemeat?" she said.

"Of course."

"One year he didn't bring it," she said to me.

"That must have been really awful," I said.

Nicholas stifled a laugh. Grandma just looked at me. "Who are you?"

"I'm Elise."

"You his wife?"

"No. We're just friends."

"There's nothing wrong with marriage," she

said. "No one gets married these days. Why would they buy the cow when the milk's free?"

"Grandma," Sharon said from the kitchen. "That's enough."

"It's nice to meet you," I said.

"It's time to eat?" she said back.

"She said *meet,*" Nicholas clarified.

"We got a turkey," she said. "That's all the meat we need." She turned to Sharon. "When do we eat? I haven't got all day."

"Nick," Sharon said. "Will you carve the turkey? Then we can eat. Scott, take the rolls in. Boys, stop playing that stupid game."

The boys just continued playing. Nicholas walked over to the bird. "Where's your electric knife?"

"I don't know where it went," Sharon said. "I think Scott ruined it making the boys' pinewood derby cars."

"That's possible," Scott said.

"You're going to have to do it the old-fashioned way," Sharon said.

Nicholas pulled a knife from a wooden block and began carving while I helped Sharon carry the last of the food over to the table.

"I'd have Scott do the carving," she said to me, loud enough for her husband to hear, "but he just makes a mess of it. I end up using most of it for turkey noodle soup. You'd think, being raised on a farm, he'd know how to carve a turkey."

"I know how to raise and *kill* a turkey," Scott said.

"Fortunately, this one came dead," Sharon replied. "Boys, put away the game and help Grandma to the table."

After we had all settled in at the table, Sharon and Scott held hands and Sharon said, "Nick, will you say a prayer over the food."

"I'd be happy to," he said. He took my hand, and we all bowed our heads.

"Dear Father in Heaven, we are grateful for this day to consider our blessings. We are grateful for the abundance of our lives. We are grateful to be together, safe and well. We ask a blessing to be upon this home and Scott and Sharon and their family. Please bless them for their generosity and love. We are grateful that Elise has joined us this year and ask that she might feel as blessed as she makes others feel. We ask this in the name of Jesus Christ. Amen."

I looked over at him. "Thank you. That was sweet."

"He says the best prayers," Sharon said. "That's why we always ask him to pray."

"I want turkey," Wilma said.

"Scott, get her some turkey," Sharon said. "Just white meat."

Scott was right: there was no way we were leaving the table hungry. There was turkey, cornbread stuffing, pecan-crusted candied yams, mashed potatoes and gravy, sweet corn, Parker House rolls, apple-pineapple salad, and green beans with bacon. By the time we were through eating, I was too full for pie. We all helped with the dishes. Then Nicholas said, "I think I need a walk."

"I'll join you," I said.

We retrieved our coats and went outside. The sun had just fallen below the western mountains, and we walked out into the middle of the vacant, snow-packed street. Nicholas turned to me. "Having fun?"

"Yes. They're nice people. Grandma's a hoot."

"I know. Every year they say this is her last year, but it never is. I think she'll outlive all of us. When death comes for her, she'll slap his face and tell him to get her a Dr Pepper, no ice."

I laughed. "Why do you think old age does that to people?"

"I don't know. Old age seems to make some people meaner and some sweeter. Maybe it's just an amplifier." I slipped on a patch of ice, and Nicholas grabbed my arm. I noticed that he didn't let go. "So how does this compare to your normal Thanksgiving?"

"The food is better. The company is *much* better."

"I'm sure the harem isn't the same without you."

"Dan will survive."

"So what is Dan like? Or have I crossed the line of addendum one."

"We have pretty much obliterated addendum one," I said. "How do I describe Dan?" I thought a moment then said, "His good side, he's not bad-looking and he's ambitious. He has big dreams. Not really practical ones, but big. At least he did when we were dating."

"And the dark side?"

"He's got a nasty temper and he's a narcissist. He's insecure but conceited at the same time. He's a chronic womanizer. On our wedding day he flirted with some of the guests. Probably the best compliment I could give him is that he's not my father."

"That's a short measuring stick," Nicholas said.

"It's the measuring stick life gave me," I replied. "It's funny how different kids can be from their parents."

"Like you," Nicholas said.

"Yes, but I meant Dan. Dan's father is the most humble man you'll ever meet. He's had his same job as a hospital administrator for more than thirty years. He adores his wife and treats her like a queen. Sometimes I wish I had married Dan's father instead of him."

"No you don't," Nicholas said. "He's too old."

I smiled. "You're right." I breathed the cold air

in deeply. "Now, may I ask you a deep, probing question?"

"It's only fair," he said.

"Do you ever wish you were married and had children?"

He thought a moment. "Yes. To both."

"Then why don't you? It's not like that would be hard for you. Just in my office I know two women who would be more than happy to oblige you."

"I guess it's just taken me a little while to get to this place."

"So why the contract? Why not just date?"

"Training wheels," he replied.

"Training wheels," I repeated, smiling. "I like that." I slipped again. Again Nicholas caught me.

"It's the shoes," I said. "They don't do snow."

"I think *you* need training wheels."

"I think you're right."

"Let's go back and have some of that pie," he said.

"All right. Just don't let me fall."

By the time we returned from our walk, the boys had disappeared and Grandma Wilma had already eaten her sliver of mincemeat and retired to the guest room to nap. Nicholas and I joined Scott and Sharon at the table for coffee and pie.

"Elise," Sharon said. "Your pies are divine. This pecan pie is amazing."

"Thank you," I said.

"You're definitely on our guest list next year."

"Or at least your pies are," Scott joked. "In case this doesn't work out."

I furtively glanced at Nicholas, who didn't respond.

We sat around and talked for nearly an hour. Eventually our conversation turned to the natural sleep agent properties of tryptophan in turkey, to which Nicholas yawned and said, "I need a nap." He looked at me as if seeking permission.

"Go for it," I said.

He went into the living room, leaving the three of us still at the table.

"The food was really great," I said to Sharon. "Thank you for letting me join you."

"Thank you for coming," Sharon said. "You know, you're good for him."

Scott nodded. "In all the years I've known Nick, I've never seen him this happy."

"We've only known each other for three weeks," I said.

"And the last three weeks he's been a changed man," Scott said.

Sharon nodded. "He's definitely in love."

The word paralyzed me. The L word. I suddenly wished that Nicholas had told them the truth about us.

"I think I'll check on Nicholas," I said. I pushed back from the table and went into the living room.

The light was off, and the room was lit by the orange-yellow fire.

Nicholas was asleep on the sofa in front of the fireplace. I sat down next to the couch and just looked at him, the flickering flames reflecting off his face. He was beautiful. More beautiful since I'd gotten to know him. *Do I really make him happy? Why does our relationship feel so real?* I took a deep breath. An inner voice said to me, *You're losing it, Elise. You know it's not real. You're going to get your heart broken.* Then another voice said back, *I don't care.* I lay my head against him and closed my eyes and pretended that we were the couple everyone thought we were.

# Chapter Fourteen

*Cars are remarkable machines. A man
may devote his life to charity, but put
him in a car and take his parking stall
and he'll cut your throat.*

### Elise Dutton's Diary

I woke the next morning to my phone ringing.
It was still dark outside.

"Hello?" I said groggily.

"What are you doing?" Nicholas asked.

"I'm sleeping. What time is it?"

"Six. Almost."

"Why are you calling me so early?"

"It's Black Friday," he said. "I need to do some
Christmas shopping. Want to come?"

"Is this on our schedule?"

"No, I'm completely ad-libbing here."

"Can I get ready first?"

"Of course. I'll be over in twenty minutes."

"Okay," I said. "Wait, I can't be ready in twenty
minutes."

"How long do you need?"

"Give me an hour."

"That's a lot of daylight," he said.

"I need an hour," I said firmly.

"All right. See you in an hour. Bye."

"Bye." I hung up, then climbed out of bed and took a shower to wake myself up. As usual, Nicholas was right on time.

"Where are we going?" I asked with my eyes closed, reclining the seat in his car.

"City Creek Center."

"It's going to be a zoo."

"I know," he said.

A few minutes later I asked, "Why aren't you tired?"

"It's a day off. Do you really want to sleep through it?"

"Yes," I said.

The shopping center was crazy crowded, and parking was at a premium. We passed two people trying to pull into the same slot in the parking garage, both unwilling to yield. They just kept honking at each other.

"Think we'll find a space?" I asked.

"I'd bet on it," he said. A few minutes later he pulled into a reserved spot with his name on it, and we took the elevator up to the ground level.

The shopping center had only opened the previous year and was clearly the place to go. It was an upscale, open-air shopping center that had a simulated creek running through it. It occupied six acres in downtown Salt Lake City with a sky bridge over Main Street connecting the two blocks.

We were walking out of Godiva Chocolatier, where we had stopped for chocolate-covered strawberries (which was probably the best breakfast I'd had in years), when Nicholas said, "I need to stop at the Coach store to pick up a bag for one of the partners. Do you mind?"

"Of course not." I followed him to the shop.

A professional-looking man, bald with a graying goatee, approached Nicholas. "May I help you, sir?"

"I'm looking for a leather carry-on bag."

"I've got just the thing," said the man. He led us over to a wall display of leather bags. "I've got the Thompson foldover tote, that's been quite popular. And the new Bleecker line. I've got the map bag in leather; it comes in two colors, brass and mahogany, and a leather-trimmed webbing strap."

"No, it looks too much like a man purse," Nicholas said. "How much is this bag?" he asked, lifting one to examine it more closely.

"That's the Bleecker flight bag. It's four hundred and ninety-eight dollars."

That was almost my entire life savings.

"What colors does it come in?" Nicholas asked.

"Just what you see here, black and brass."

"I'll take the brass."

"Very good choice," the man said. "Much more masculine design. Do you need anything else?"

"No, that's all."

"Give me just a moment and I'll ring you up."

"Here's my card," Nicholas said, handing him a black credit card. There was a long line of people making purchases.

"That's a nice bag," I said.

"It's for one of my partners," he said. "He'll like it. He likes luggage."

"It's expensive."

"Not for him," he said.

"Or you," I added. As we waited in line I noticed that there was a Pandora shop across the way. Cathy was a Pandora fanatic, and she always loved getting new charms.

"Nicholas," I said, "I'm going to go over to the Pandora shop."

"No problem. I'll come over after."

I walked over to the store and browsed the display cases until I found a sterling silver clover with green enamel. It was perfect. Cathy was Irish and proud of it.

"May I help you?" a woman asked. I looked up. The woman was about my age, heavy with gold, permed hair.

"I'd like to purchase that charm right there," I said, pointing to the piece.

"The clover?" she asked.

"Yes, please."

She lifted it from the display case. "This also comes in gold with diamonds."

"The silver charm is fine, thank you."

"Anything else?"

"No, that's it."

"This way, please."

I followed her over to the cash register.

"Will that be cash or plastic?"

"Plastic," I said, handing her my Visa card. She ran my card, glanced at the name, then back up at me. "Do I know you?"

"I don't think so."

She glanced once more at my name on the credit card. "Elise Dutton. No, I think I do. What school did you go to?"

"I'm not from around here."

"Hmm," she said, handing me back my card. Then a look of recognition came to her eyes. "I know who you are. I read a story about you a few years back. You . . ." She stopped abruptly.

"Yes?" I said.

"I'm sorry," she said. "I'm mistaken."

She quickly packaged up my purchase and handed me the bag. "Thank you for shopping. Have a good day."

"Happy holidays," I said dully, then quickly left the store.

Nicholas met me as I was walking out. "Sorry that took so long," he said. "That guy was inept

132

with a cash register." He looked at me closely. "Are you okay?"

"I'm not feeling well," I said. "Can we go?"

"Of course." He glanced over at the store, then took my hand. "Come on. It's too crowded here anyway."

# Chapter Fifteen

*Dan came to see me today. He's about as welcome as a January utility bill.*

## Elise Dutton's Diary

The next Monday was calmer than usual since we didn't have any tours out that week. The holidays were our slowest time of the year, and most of our efforts then went toward preparing and marketing the next year's tours.

A little before noon I looked up to see Dan standing in the doorway of my office. "Flowers," he said. "Where'd you get those?"

"What do you want?" I asked.

He stepped into my office. "You weren't at Thanksgiving dinner."

"I told your parents I wouldn't be there."

"You didn't tell me."

"What do you want, Dan?"

"I came to see what's up. Why you didn't come."

"I was busy."

"On Thanksgiving?"

"Is that so hard to believe?"

"What, you had work?"

"I had another invitation to dinner," I said, annoyed by his persistence. "I always thought it was weird anyway, going to dinner with you and Kayla."

"An invitation from who?"

"A friend."

"A friend," he said suspiciously. "Male or female?"

"I don't need to report to you."

"A man, huh?" He walked closer to my desk. "Tell you what—I'll take you to lunch, and you can tell me about this guy. I'll pay." He made the offer sound remarkably magnanimous, and, for him, it was.

"I already have lunch plans," I said.

"Since when do you have lunch plans?"

"Since when do you care?" I said. "Where's Kayla? Why don't you take her to lunch?"

"I need to talk to you about her," he said. "Who are you lunching with?"

"A friend," I said.

"The Thanksgiving guy?"

"That's none of your business."

"What's Thanksgiving guy's name?"

"Nicholas," Nicholas said, walking into my office.

Dan turned around. The look on his face was priceless, a mix of surprise and fear.

"Hi, Elise," Nicholas said. He leaned forward and kissed me on the cheek.

Dan glanced back and forth between us, still not sure how to react.

"This is Dan," I said. "My ex-husband."

Nicholas looked at him coolly. "Dan."

"Whassup," Dan said. I knew Dan well enough to know that he was intimidated. Subconsciously, he threw his chest out a little.

Nicholas turned back to me. "Are you ready?"

"Yes." I took his hand. "I'll talk to you later," I said to Dan.

"Yeah, whatever," Dan said.

Nicholas and I walked out of my office, leaving Dan standing there alone. I should have known that he'd never leave my new relationship alone.

# Chapter Sixteen

*Dan's the kid in the sandbox who
always wants the toy someone else has.*

## Elise Dutton's Diary

Dan was waiting on the landing outside my apartment when I got home from work.

"Whassup?" he said as I approached. "I was just in the area, thought I'd stop by."

"What were you doing in the area?" I asked. I unlocked the door and walked in.

"I came to see you." He followed me inside, took off his coat, and threw it, then himself, on my couch. "So how was your date?"

"What date?"

"The one I caught you on. With what's-his-name."

"You didn't *catch* me," I said. "And don't act childish. You know his name."

"Dick?"

I didn't answer.

"Dickolaus."

I just glared at him.

"Whatever. The Nick-man. So where'd you meet him?"

"In the food court."

"Oh, that's cool."

"*We* met in a Laundromat," I said. "What does that make us?"

"Divorced," Dan said. "So what, he's like your boyfriend now?"

"Something like that. What's it to you?"

"Kayla's gone."

"Gone where?"

"She cheated on me. With some old rich guy."

"Am I supposed to feel bad for you?"

"Would it kill you to show a little sympathy?"

"She's a cheater, what did you expect?"

"I expected she would be loyal."

"Like you?"

"I was loyal to *her*."

*For a change,* I thought. I breathed out in exasperation. "What do you want, Dan?"

"I want you. I want us to be like we were."

"That ship has sailed," I said.

"You didn't give me a chance. I stuck by you when you screwed up, but I slip up and you're gone."

"*You* didn't stick by me. You divorced *me*."

"Only because you were going to divorce me."

"I never said I was going to divorce you. I should have, but I never did."

"But you were *going* to."

"You don't know that. I don't even know that, which is pathetic, since you were cheating on me with my best friend while I was in the ICU clinging to life."

He looked at me for a moment and his voice softened. "Elise, it's always been us. We understand each other. We've been through the storms together. We should be together. You know it."

"I believed that once," I said. "I don't anymore."

"Why, because some rich lawyer comes knocking at your door? He's probably married."

"No, he's not married. Not everyone cheats like you, Dan."

"A lot more than you think. How long have you known him?"

"A few weeks."

"I don't trust him."

"You don't know him well enough to not trust him."

"Neither do you."

I groaned with exasperation. "I'm not having this conversation. You need to leave."

"Come on, 'Lise. We match. Just admit it. If we didn't, then why did you marry me?"

"I was desperate."

"No, you believed in us. And you were right. Drop the lawyer and I'll move in with you."

"It's not going to happen, Dan. Now you need to go. I have to go grocery shopping."

He grabbed his coat and smiled. "You'll come around," he said. "Like a boomerang. You'll think about it, then you'll see the light. Who else knows everything about you? You know how people are when they learn about . . ."

"About what?"

"You know. Hannah."

"Get out," I said.

He remained undaunted. "See you later, 'Lise." He stepped across the threshold, then said, "Boomerang."

I shut the door after him. As much as I hated hearing it from him, Dan was right. Whenever people made the connection between me and the woman in the newspaper who killed her daughter, they just mysteriously disappeared. I leaned against the door and cried.

# Chapter Seventeen

*The annual ICE Christmas affair is about as classy as a truck pull, but without the dress code.*

## ELISE DUTTON'S DIARY

The ICE Christmas party was a perennial redux—a potluck affair that was always held at my boss's home in Olympus Cove. He lived in a Tudor-style house decorated with plastic reindeer in the front yard and a fake plastic chimney on the roof with Santa's boots extending straight up as if he were stuck.

Nicholas had picked me up along with my pomegranate-and-poppy-seed-dressed salad. I brought the same salad every year, and took it home every year barely eaten, since most of the office avoided salad like a toxin. Still, Mark insisted that I bring it because his wife, Shelley, once remarked that she liked it. I had since concluded that she was only being polite since she hadn't eaten any of it for the last two years.

Nicholas parked his BMW across the street from the house, and I carried my bowl up to the door.

"Shall I ring the bell?" Nicholas asked.

"No. They won't answer; just walk in."

He opened the door. As I anticipated, there was no one to greet us, and the only sounds came from the television in the family room.

"I'll take your coat," Nicholas said.

I set my salad on the floor, then took off my coat and handed it to him. "They put them in the living room," I said.

Nicholas added our coats to a pile of outerwear already covering the crushed-velvet sofa. Then we walked into the kitchen. No one noticed (or cared) as I lay my salad on the counter.

My boss, Mark Engeman, was notoriously tight-fisted, and the party's food was grocery store platters of meat and cheese laid out next to plates of Ritz and saltine crackers dressed with cheese from a can. There were also jalapeño poppers, store-bought rolls to make sandwiches, and a large bowl of carrot-raisin salad, which was always Cathy's contribution.

The one place Mark splurged was on beer. His refrigerator was stocked with all the Budweiser it could hold. There was also a plastic cooler filled with beer. I think he caught on that his guests rated the party by the level of intoxication they achieved, which was just one of many reasons that I was always the first to leave.

Everyone else was already there. Mark and his wife, Shelley; Cathy, who brought Maureen, her snarky sister. And Brent and Margaret, our two group escorts, whom we rarely saw because they were on the road more than two hundred days out of the year, with their spouses.

Closest to the kitchen were Zoey and her date. As usual, Zoey had brought someone none of us had ever seen and would likely never see again, which made introductory conversation pointless. Her boy du jour was tall and muscular, handsome but not especially bright-looking. He wore a sleeveless Utah Jazz jersey, which emphasized his biceps and myriad tattoos but seemed out of place considering the abundance of snow outside.

With the exception of Shelley and Margaret, everyone was sitting around the living room eating nachos and watching the Jazz play the Portland Trail Blazers. They had all gotten an early start on drinking, and empty beer cans littered the coffee table that three of them had their feet on. Cathy was the first to notice us. "Elise. Nicholas," she said. "You made it."

Everyone looked over.

"Hi, everyone," I said.

Nicholas looked as unsure of himself as he had when he first approached me in the food court.

"Hey," Mark said. "Help yourself to a beer. Got Bud in the fridge."

"Thank you," Nicholas said, making no movement to act on the offer.

"Come watch the game," Zoey said.

"Go ahead, sit," I said to Nicholas. "I'll get us some food."

Nicholas sat down on a chair next to the others. Zoey was holding an open beer. She already looked a little buzzed. She almost immediately leaned toward Nicholas, drawn like steel to a magnet. I walked to the kitchen table and began making ham and cheese sandwiches.

"Thanks for all the gifts you've been sending," Zoey said to him. "Especially the cheesecake. It was *dreamy*."

"I'm glad you liked it," Nicholas said casually, politely glancing at her before looking back at the television. "What quarter are we in?" he asked.

"Just started the third," Mark said. "You ever watch the Jazz play?"

"Sometimes. We've got box seats," he said. "At the firm."

"And you're a partner, right?" Zoey asked rhetorically.

"Yes."

Zoey's date just stared ahead at the screen, sucking on a beer, completely oblivious to her obvious interest in my date.

I walked back over with our food. "Here you

go," I said, handing Nicholas a plate with some of my salad and a sandwich. I sat down between Nicholas and Zoey.

"Thank you," Nicholas said, turning all his attention to me. For the next hour we just watched the game, which the Jazz ended up losing by four points.

"They never lose when I wear this shirt," Zoey's date said angrily.

"Are you ready to go?" I asked Nicholas.

"Whatever you want," he said.

"I'm ready."

"Okay," he said. "I'll get the coats." He walked out of the room.

Zoey stood and walked out after him. I also stood up and walked out, stopping in the hall just outside the living room. I could hear Zoey talking. "So where did you and Elise meet?"

"We just bumped into each other. In the building."

"I'm in the building," she said. There was a short pause, then she added, "I'm sorry we never bumped into each other. I mean, before you two." There was another pause. "Is it serious? You and Elise."

"You mean, would I be interested in exploring other romantic possibilities?"

"You're so smart," she said. "Yes. I mean, hypo"—she struggled with the word—"hypo, hypothetically."

"That's a big word," Nicholas said.

"I'm not dumb," she said. "Maybe a little drunk."

"Hypothetically, no. I wouldn't. And you better get back to your date."

"He's an idiot," she said.

"We'll just keep that to ourselves," Nicholas replied.

I wasn't surprised by Zoey's antics, but I was still angry. I walked into the room glaring at her. "Let's get out of here," I said to Nicholas.

Zoey was either too drunk or too dumb to realize that I'd been listening. "Bye, Elise," she said.

I didn't answer her. I was fuming.

Nicholas took my arm. "Let's go home."

I didn't say much on the way back to my apartment. Nicholas must have known how I was feeling because he didn't pry. It had started snowing, and the BMW's windshield wipers kept beat to the Christmas songs on the radio. The cheerful tunes were completely incongruent with the thoughts running through my head, which were definitely not peace on earth goodwill to men.

Outside my apartment door Nicholas asked, "Are you okay?"

I blew up. "I can't believe she hit on you."

"Yes you can," he said calmly. "She was drunk."

"She would have done it anyway."

"Maybe."

"Why are you defending her?"

"I'm not. But don't go too hard on her. If she was happy with her life, she wouldn't have come after me. *And* she'd been drinking."

I took a deep breath. "I don't have to like her."

"No. But you do have to work with her. So you might as well keep things civil."

"Civil," I said angrily. "I want to pluck her eyelashes."

Nicholas laughed. "Promise me you won't do that. Or anything else. Just let it go."

"But she's a—"

He put a finger to my lips. "This is for your good," he said. "Trust me. Promise me."

Honestly, I liked that he was touching my lips. "All right," I finally said. "Why do you have to be so rational?"

"It's a habit."

After a moment I said, "May I ask you something?"

"Of course."

"If it wasn't for the contract, would you have hooked up with her?"

"No."

"Why not? Everyone else wants to."

"She's not my type."

"What's your type?"

He just smiled. "Let me know when you figure that out." He kissed me on the cheek. "Good night, Elise. I enjoyed being with you." He started to walk away, then stopped and turned back. "Oh, do you know what today is?"

"No."

"It's our midpoint. We're halfway through our contract." He turned and walked away.

I watched him walk out to his car before going inside. His final words hurt my heart even more than Zoey's betrayal.

# Chapter Eighteen

*Everyone has a dark and light side.
How much we see of either is usually
less a matter of the moon's position
than where we're standing.*

## ELISE DUTTON'S DIARY

In spite of my promise to Nicholas, the next day at work I treated Zoey coldly. I was still angry, hurt, and jealous, a perfect storm of emotion. Even if Nicholas wasn't really mine, Zoey didn't know that. She had scores of men and she went after mine. I'd never forgive her for being so cruel.

A little before noon Zoey brought a package into my office. "Here's your present," she said softly.

I glanced up only for a second, then went back to my work. "Just put it on the chair."

"Okay," she said. She didn't leave my office.

After a minute I said, "Do you need something?"

"Elise, I'm sorry."

"For what?" I asked innocently, forcing her confession.

"I had too much to drink last night and I hit on Nicholas at the party. I feel really bad."

"Why would you do that to me?" I asked, unleashing my anger. "What have I ever done to you?"

"I'm so sorry." Her eyes began welling up with tears. She wiped at them. "I'm an idiot, I know it. And just so you know, Nick didn't go for it for a second. He's completely loyal to you."

I still wasn't in a mood to forgive her, so I didn't say anything. Zoey started crying in earnest. She continued. "When I got home I was really mad at myself. I thought, *What's wrong with me? Why would I do that? Elise is such a good person.*" She grabbed a Kleenex from my desk. "The thing is, I'm just really insecure inside. I have this need to prove myself. It's like . . ." She shook her head. "This isn't coming out right." She took a deep breath, then said, "I'm sorry, okay? I'm just really jealous of you. Because, Nick is really great and he really loves you, and the guys I meet just love my body and the way I look and no one wants to keep me, they just want to use me. But Nick loves all of you. Inside and out. And you deserve that. You deserve a nice guy like him. You really do." I couldn't believe that Zoey was jealous of me. She looked at me, then said, "I'll quit bothering you. But I'm sorry." She turned to go.

"Zoey," I said.

She slowly turned back, wiping her eyes.

"I understand."

"You do?"

"I didn't know you felt that way. I've judged you wrong. I'm sorry."

After a minute she said, "Can I give you a hug?"

"Yes."

I stood while Zoey came around my desk and put her arms around me. "I'll never do that again," she said. "I promise."

"I know you won't."

"If I can do anything to make it up to you, just ask."

I looked at her a moment before asking, "Do you really mean that?"

She nodded.

"I have some parties coming up with Nicholas, and I don't have anything to wear."

"You want to borrow my clothes?"

"Right," I said. "I couldn't fit this body into anything you own. But I'm not good with fashion. I've been out of the game for too long. And everyone he works with is rich and cool."

She suddenly smiled. "You want me to dress you?"

"If you would."

"I'd love to."

"I don't have much money."

"We don't need money," she said. "I have friends. Can I work on your hair too?"

"Yes."

"We'll knock Nicholas off his feet," she said. "I mean, you will. I'll just help you."

"Thank you."

"When's your next party?"

"Saturday night."

"This Saturday?"

I nodded.

"Okay. I hope your Saturday is open, because we've got some work to do."

# Chapter Nineteen

*Nicholas is like a golden ticket.*

## ELISE DUTTON'S DIARY

December first. Exactly one month since Nicholas had approached me in the food court. Zoey arrived at my apartment Saturday afternoon with a pile of dress bags, two large makeup boxes, a jewelry box, four shoe boxes, and a canvas bag filled with hair supplies. It took us three trips to get everything in from her car.

She had found me four dresses, all on "loan" from Nordstrom, where one of her ex-boyfriends was a manager. There were also several sets of matching jewelry for each dress.

All the dresses Zoey brought were stunning. I tried them all on, and Zoey snapped pictures of me with her phone. It took us an hour to settle on two. The one I would wear that night at the firm party was a black, form-fitting crepe sheath with a sheer top.

The other dress was the most expensive of the

four: a one-shoulder nude evening gown with beads. I decided to save it for the partners' party, because we guessed it would be the fanciest of Nicholas's events.

We looked through her boxes of shoes, and for the first dress I chose a simple but elegant pair of black patent leather pumps. For the partners' party I chose a glittery pair of peep-toed high heels. Then we chose earrings and necklaces for both dresses.

With the dresses and accessories selected, we took a break and drove to the nearest Starbucks for a latte. After we got back we discussed my general look, experimenting with different shades of makeup for almost an hour. As Zoey worked on my makeup, she taught me some new techniques.

"You *can* teach an old dog new tricks," I said.

Zoey stepped back to look at me. "You're not *old,* and you're not a *dog*. Never, ever call yourself that."

"I was just joking," I said.

"Especially joking," she said. "Your subconscious mind doesn't know the difference. You need to be your own best cheerleader."

I was impressed by her counsel. There was a lot more to Zoey than I'd given her credit for.

Sitting in my kitchen, Zoey wasn't the same girl I knew in the office. She was much more funny, relaxed, and vulnerable. She was also sweet. She kept telling me that with my natural beauty I didn't need a makeover, just a few enhancements. "You don't make over gorgeous," she said.

I hadn't had a girlfriend since Kayla had betrayed me, and it was wonderful to have female companionship again. I wondered if, in spite of the age difference, Zoey and I might be friends. Nicholas had brought me out of my cave, and I was going to need someone to do things with after our contract expired.

Zoey worked on my hair for over an hour and experimented with several shades of lipstick before finding the right one. Finally, she stepped back and scrutinized me like a sculptor examining her creation. She nodded, then said, "Oh my, Elise. You should look at yourself."

I walked out to the hall mirror. I couldn't believe it. "I look pretty," I said.

"No, you look *hot*. He's in serious trouble."

While I was helping her pack up her things, Zoey said, "You and Nick are such a great couple. If you want, I'll help you with your makeup at your wedding."

I wasn't sure what to say. Finally I said, "I would like that."

Zoey left just a few minutes before Nicholas arrived. He rang the doorbell at seven. "Come in," I shouted, wanting to present myself properly.

He let himself in. "Hi, it's me."

"I'll be out in just a minute. Help yourself to the fridge. I think there's some soda and juice."

A moment later he said, "There's something green in a blender pitcher. Is it supposed to be green?"

"It's not mold," I said. "It just looks like it. That's my kale drink."

"Looks like kale," he said, which sounded like 'Looks like hell,' which I think was his intent. "How was your day?"

"Good."

"What did you do?"

"Not much," I said. "Zoey came over."

"After the other night, I'm surprised that you two are talking."

"She apologized for coming on to you."

I spritzed myself with perfume, took a good look at myself, then walked out into my front room. Nicholas was sitting on my couch. He immediately stood. "Wow."

"What?" I asked innocently.

"You look amazing."

I smiled. "Shall we go?"


Nicholas's office party was held each year at La Caille, an expensive French restaurant tucked away on a twenty-acre reserve at the mouth of Little Cottonwood Canyon. I had been to the restaurant only once before, for a wedding of one of Dan's co-workers, and I had never forgotten it. Housed in a stucco, ivy-covered French château, it had its own three-acre vineyard, and during the warmer months peacocks roamed the yard amid statuary and topiaries, while black and white swans glided in the swan pool. Tonight, the grounds were covered in snow and were extravagantly lit with strings of white lights.

Nicholas pulled his car up the restaurant's tree-lined cobblestone drive to a roundabout near the front door. He handed his keys to the valet, then took my arm and led me inside. The lobby was exquisite, with a large antique chandelier and parquet-tile floor. Harpsichord music softly echoed through the tile and stucco interior.

The young hostess who greeted us looked like a model, and, as I remembered from the wedding, all the waitresses wore low-cut gowns that were presumably all the rage in eighteenth-century France.

"Your firm rents the entire restaurant?" I asked.

"Every year," Nicholas said.

"What does that cost?"

"Enough," he said with a pained smile.

We walked up a circular stairway to the main dining room, which was crowded with several hundred of the firm's staff and guests. Everyone seemed pleased to see Nicholas.

"You're very popular," I said.

"Of course," he said. "I'm a partner. I help decide

what they get paid. Would you like something to drink? They have remarkable eggnog."

"I would love an eggnog," I said.

"Coming up."

While I was waiting for Nicholas to return, a stunningly attractive woman in an eggplant-colored strapless evening gown walked up to me. "Hi, I'm Candace," she said.

"Hi. I'm Elise."

"You're Nick's girlfriend."

"I . . ." I smiled. "Yes."

"It's nice to meet you." Something about the way she said it made me doubt her sincerity.

"Are you a legal secretary at the firm?" I asked.

She practically grimaced with disgust. "No, I'm a lawyer," she said. "And what is it that you do?"

"I'm in travel," I said.

"Travel," she repeated lightly. "I avoid it if I can. I'm a diamond-level frequent flier with Delta."

"That's way too much time in the air," I said.

"You're telling me," she replied. "How did you and Nicholas meet?"

"We just started talking in the food court."

"The food court. At the office?"

"I know. Not very romantic."

"I guess I need to start eating more fast food. This Paleo diet certainly isn't doing anything for me."

"I would disagree," I said. "You look gorgeous."

She seemed surprised by the compliment. "Thank you."

Just then Nicholas returned, carrying two glasses. "Hello, Candace," he said.

Both her expression and her body language changed as if someone had flipped a switch. "Hello, Nicholas."

Nicholas handed me my drink. "One eggnog."

"Thank you," I said.

"Candace is one of our more successful litigators," Nicholas said.

"What he really means is that I have more billable hours than most."

"That too," he said, smiling.

She took a step toward him. "I heard about the Bellagio case. That should be interesting."

"I might have to make a few research trips to Las Vegas."

"Oh, that sounds painful. If you need any backup, I'd be happy to help."

"Thanks for the offer," he said.

"Think about it," she said. "Have a good night." She glanced at me once more, then said rather stiffly, "It was nice to meet you, Alicia." She turned and walked off.

I stood there, a little stunned.

"Sorry about that, Alicia," Nicholas said.

"Was that intentional?"

"Probably." He took my arm. "Come on, let me introduce you to some of the others."

I followed Nicholas from one side of the restaurant to the other as he shook hands and introduced me to what seemed like a hundred strangers. Near the center of the room I was glad to see Scott and Sharon Hitesman. While Nicholas and Scott talked, Sharon sidled up to me.

"Elise, you look stunning."

"Thank you. And thank you again for letting me crash your Thanksgiving dinner."

"You have no idea how glad I was to finally see Nicholas with someone. He deserves someone like you."

"Someone like me?" I said.

She smiled at me. "Someone who makes him happy."

A minute later Nicholas returned to my side to resume our tour of the floor. He was definitely well liked. And, with the exception of Candace's snub, everyone was friendly.

"Hungry?" Nicholas asked.

"I'm starving."

"Me too. Enough of this obligatory socializing, let's eat."

Like the surroundings, the fare was extravagant —the opposite of my office party. Actually, everything was the opposite of my office party. Instead of a plastic Tupperware bowl filled with ice and beer, there were silver ice buckets with expensive wines and a large ice sculpture of a swan.

"It's not Cafe Rio," Nicholas said, "but it's edible."

"It may surprise you, but I actually eat more than Cafe Rio."

"Yes, I've seen you eat turkey," he said. "And steak. And Chinese food."

"And Thai," I added.

"I think I'm getting through to you," he said, setting some shrimp on his plate. "I love shrimp."

"I love shrimp, too," I said.

"I'll get enough for both of us." He loaded up his own plate, then pointed at some other things for me to get. Salmon on rice, roast chicken, crab-stuffed mushrooms, quiche, Brie and pâté de foie gras with crackers, chocolate-dipped strawberries, and puff pastries shaped like swans.

We carried our plates up the stairs to a small dining room where there was only one other couple. Nicholas found us a quiet place tucked in the corner behind the servers' station.

"So what do you think of our party?"

"I feel a little out of place," I said. "Everything is so nice."

"You deserve nice," he said. "Thank you for coming with me. Usually I just put in my time, eat a few shrimp, and bolt. It's been really nice having you here."

"I think everyone's fooled," I said.

"What do you mean?"

"They really think we're a couple."

He ate a few more shrimp, then said, "You know what's sad is that we might be one of the most authentic couples here tonight."

"What do you mean?"

"Charles, Blake, and Stephanie are having affairs. Phil and his paralegal Rachel have mysteriously disappeared at the same time every Thursday afternoon for the last three years, and Kurt is waiting for the optimum financial opportunity to divorce his wife. What we have might be more real than much of what we saw out there tonight."

"Are Scott and Sharon happy?"

"Yes. They're the real thing."

"They seem happy," I said.

Nicholas must have tired of the topic because he took a drink of eggnog and said, "I know I said it before, but you really do look beautiful tonight."

"It's the dress."

"That's like saying the *Mona Lisa* is beautiful because of its frame."

We stole off from the party without saying good-bye. Nicholas took the long way back to my place, which I didn't mind. I didn't want the night to end. It was almost midnight when he pulled up in front of my apartment.

"I hope that wasn't too painful," he said.

"No. It was really nice. Actually, I haven't been

anywhere that nice for a long time. They treated me better than my own colleagues."

"You can accuse us lawyers of many things, but we are civil. At least most of the time. Candace could have been nicer."

"I'm afraid I drew first blood."

"How's that?"

"I asked her if she was a legal secretary."

Nicholas grimaced. "Yes, that would definitely pull her chain."

"I'm sorry," I said.

"It's all right. She'll get over it." He leaned over and kissed me on the cheek. "Good night, Elise."

"Good night." I reached for the door handle, then looked back. "May I ask you something?"

"Of course."

"Why are you so nice to me?"

He was quiet a moment, then said, "It makes me sad that you had to ask."

I didn't know what to say to that. "Good night, Nicholas. Thank you for a lovely evening."

"It was my pleasure."

That night as I lay alone in bed thinking about how nice the evening had been, a terrible thought crossed my mind. *Maybe I shouldn't have signed the contract after all.* Sometimes it's just better not to know what you're missing.

# Chapter Twenty

*Something is wrong with Nicholas.*
*I wish I knew what to do.*

## ELISE DUTTON'S DIARY

For the first time since I'd started working at ICE, I found myself looking forward to Monday. More specifically, seeing Nicholas. And I loved anticipating his gifts. I don't know how he kept up with them. Though I suspected his secretary helped with them, I was sure that he picked them out himself. Monday I got a candle scented like Christmas sugar cookies, on Tuesday a DVD of *A Christmas Carol* (the George C. Scott version of course), and on Wednesday a CD of a Kenny G Christmas album.

On Thursday the sixth, something changed. There was no gift. And Nicholas was different. He was tense and withdrawn. He wasn't just acting different, he looked different. At lunch he barely ate. He barely spoke. He barely even looked at me. I wondered if I'd done something to upset him.

Finally, I asked, "Is something wrong at work?"

"No," he said darkly. "Same old tricks. People suing each other, divorcing each other, contesting wills, brother against brother, sister against sister, everyone looking out for themselves." He shook his head with disgust. "As if there weren't already enough pain in this godforsaken world."

The tone of his voice frightened me. After a moment I asked, "Are you okay?"

He pushed his salad around a little, then looked up. "I'm fine."

"You're not yourself today."

"It's nothing," he said.

We sat quietly for a moment until I said, "If I did something . . ."

"It's nothing," he repeated sharply.

Emotion rose in my chest. "I'm sorry," I said. I stood. "I better go."

He likewise stood, reaching for my arm. "No, please. I'm sorry. I didn't mean that." He hesitated for a moment, then said, "I'm just under a lot of pressure. I'm really sorry I snapped. Please . . . forgive me."

I looked into his anxious eyes. It was more than stress. There was pain in them. "Okay." We both sat back down. After a moment I said, "It's not your fault. I kept pushing you. I was afraid that maybe I'd done something wrong."

He looked at me for a moment, then said, "It's not you."

"If I can do anything to make you feel better . . ."

He reached across the table and took my hand. "If there were something anyone could do, you would be the one I'd go to. I'll be okay. I promise. I go through this every year around this time. It will pass."

I wondered what he'd meant by that, but I wasn't about to ask. We sat there for a few more minutes eating in awkward silence. I wasn't really hungry anymore, and there didn't seem to be much more to say. "I guess I better let you go," I said.

He looked sad. "I'm sorry I wasn't better company." We both stood. "I'll see you on Monday." He turned to go.

"Nicholas," I said. I walked up to him and put my arms around him. "I don't know what's going on. But I care." I hugged him tighter.

When I stepped back, I noticed that his eyes were slightly red. "Thank you," he said softly. "That means more than you know." He turned and walked away.

The next day I didn't leave my office at lunchtime, which everyone noticed.

"Where's Nick?" Zoey asked.

"He's out of town," I said, not really knowing where he was. It just seemed the best way to explain why I wasn't with him.

"Good. Then you can come to lunch with us," Zoey said. "Cathy and I are going to get sushi."

"Thanks," I said. "But I'm not hungry."

Zoey touched my arm. "Are you okay?"

"Nicholas is just acting a little different."

She nodded. "It will be okay. Sometimes men just need some space. Some cave time."

I forced a smile. "I'm sure you're right." Inside I wasn't sure.

I worried about Nicholas all weekend. I wanted to call him, but never did. Maybe it was just fear, but something told me not to. Our time apart revealed to me just how much I cared about him and needed him. I was beginning to fear Christmas.

# Chapter Twenty-one

*When I signed the contract I knew the relationship was fake. So why doesn't it feel that way anymore?*

## ELISE DUTTON'S DIARY

I was anxious from the moment I woke on Monday. For the first time since I'd signed the contract I was nervous to see Nicholas. My anxiety grew as lunchtime neared.

About a half hour before noon Mark walked into my office. "We've got a problem," he said. "The Marriott you booked in New York for our Dayton group has a gas leak and had to evacuate. We've got sixty kids on a bus and no place to stay for the night."

I groaned. "All right. I'll get on the phone." I pulled up my list of New York hotels and began calling. Nicholas called from the food court at a quarter after noon. I had been so involved in my crisis that I hadn't realized what time it was.

"You're standing me up?" he asked.

"I'm sorry, I didn't realize it was so late."

"Then I'll wait," he said.

"No, I can't come."

"Then you *are* standing me up?"

"No, it's just, I have a problem. One of my hotels shut down, and I need to find someplace for sixty kids to stay. This might take all afternoon."

He was quiet a moment before he said, "Well, you have to eat. I'll bring something up."

"That would be great," I said.

"Pork salad?"

"Anything," I said.

Nicholas arrived about fifteen minutes later carrying a bag of food. As worried as I had been to see him, he looked fine. He set the bag on my desk. "Here you go," he said. "Change of cuisine."

"What did you get?"

"A Chick-fil-A sandwich. I figured you need something you can eat while you talk on the phone." He brought out the sandwich and a drink and laid them on my desk. "And the lemonade is sugar-free. How's it going?"

"Not well. It's hard finding a block of that many rooms last minute."

"Can I help you call?"

"Really?"

"Why not?"

"How much time do you have?"

"Maybe forty-five minutes."

"That would help." I printed off a list of hotels, then tore it in half. "Just tell them it's an emergency and ask if they have a block of thirty-two rooms, double-occupancy, for tonight."

"What if they have availability for twenty?"

"That's not enough."

"I know, but couldn't you use two hotels?"

"If we have to," I said. "But they'd have to be close to each other."

"What phone should I use?"

"There's one out in the reception area. Use line three."

"Line three," he said, walking out with the paper I'd given him. Less than a half hour later he walked back into my office. "I've got one on the line," he said. He laid the list down on my desk. "I circled it," he said. "The Liss Suites in Brooklyn."

He had doodled all over my phone list. There was a cartoon picture of a woman with her hair on fire.

"Is this supposed to be me?"

"No. Maybe."

"It looks like me."

He grinned. "It probably is."

In spite of my stress I laughed. "Okay, so did they give you a rate?"

"No. But the manager said that they'd match your rate if it was reasonable."

"You're a doll," I said. I picked up the phone

while Nicholas sat back and watched. The hotel worked out perfectly. It was actually nicer than the one I had originally reserved.

"Sounds like my work here is done," Nicholas said as I hung up.

"Thank you. Thank you."

"You're welcome."

"You're good at this. You might put me out of my job someday."

"I've been looking for something meaningful to do with my life," he said.

"You saved sixty kids from sleeping on the streets of New York."

He stood, "Sorry to save the day and run, but I need to get back to my other job."

"I'll walk you to the elevator," I said.

In the hallway he asked, "How was your weekend?"

I looked him in the eyes. "Awful." We stopped in front of the elevator.

"Why awful?"

"Because all I did was worry about you."

He was quiet a moment then said, "Thank you for worrying." He pushed the up button and said, "I told you I'd be okay."

"I know. You look much better."

"I am."

"So, I'll see you tomorrow?"

"I'm around all week. And we have the partners' party this Friday."

"When do you leave for New York?"

"Monday. Have you ever been to New York at Christmastime?"

"I've never been to New York at any time."

"Not even to check out the hotels?"

"Not even. Either Mark or one of our guides does that."

"That's a shame," he said. "There's no place like New York at Christmas. Rockefeller Center, Fifth Avenue, Radio City Music Hall. It's magical."

"Maybe someday," I said.

"Come with me next week."

"Yeah, right," I said.

He looked at me seriously. "You said we'd see how things were going. I think they're going well, don't you?"

"Yes," I said.

"Then come with me. I'll have meetings during the day, but you can go sightseeing. Then at night, we'll go out on the town. It will be fun."

"I'd have to see if I can take the time off."

"How much vacation time do you have?"

"I don't know."

"When was the last time you took a vacation?"

"I don't know."

"Exactly. Time to cash some in." When I didn't speak, he said, "Look, when are you going to get another offer for an all-expenses-paid trip to New York City?"

"I'll think about it," I said.

"All right. You think about it. But let me know soon so we can book your flight. The flights get pretty full this time of year."

"Okay," I said. "I'll let you know by tomorrow."

Just then the elevator bell rang. Zoey and Cathy stepped out.

"Hi, Nick," Zoey said. "Hi, Elise."

"Hello, ladies," Nicholas said. He leaned forward and kissed me on the cheek. "Think about it." He stepped past them into the elevator. "Have a good day."

After the door shut Zoey said, "Think about what?"

"Did he propose to you?" Cathy asked.

"No," I said. "He wants me to go to New York with him."

"At Christmas?" Zoey said. "New York is amazing at Christmas. What's there to think about?"

I thought for just a moment, then said, "You're right."

I called Nicholas just ten minutes later. "I want to go."

"Excellent," he said. "I'll have Sabrina book the flight."

"How long will we be there?"

"All week," he said.

"I'm so excited."

"Me too," he said. "You're going to love it."

# Chapter Twenty-two

*Tonight Nicholas took me to his home.*
*I would have liked to stay longer.*
*Much longer. Like forever.*

## ELISE DUTTON'S DIARY

Nicholas and I skipped lunch the next Friday because he had too much to do before leaving town. Instead I spent my lunch break with Zoey, who used the time to fix my hair for Nicholas's partners' party.

"You better take a lot of pictures tonight," she said. "I want to see you in that dress. Do you remember which earrings we picked out?"

"We put them in a Ziploc bag and wrote the date on it with a Sharpie."

She laughed. "Oh, yeah. No margin for error."

"I'm a little nervous," I said. "That first party was so fancy, but I'm afraid this one is going to be more so."

"Just have fun. You're going to be great."

"I just don't want to embarrass Nicholas in front of his partners."

"The only problem you'll have is all their wives will hate you."

"Why would they hate me?"

"Because all their husbands will be ogling you."

I smiled. I was sure Zoey had had more than her share of wife-hate.

"Speaking of ogling," she said, "have you noticed how Mark looks at you these days?"

The comment caught me off guard. "He's married."

"Yes, but he's not blind."

"Why would he suddenly notice me?"

"Probably because someone else did," she replied.

When I got home from work I took a quick shower, then put on *the dress*—the silk masterpiece Zoey and I had chosen for tonight. I had never worn anything so elegant. It hung from one shoulder, and the beads sewn into the fabric shimmered as I moved. Then I put on the jewelry that we had picked out. The earrings were larger than I was used to, but they matched the elegance of the dress. The heels I'd chosen were also taller than I usually wore, but they made a statement as well. I felt gorgeous.

Nicholas shook his head when he saw me. "Wow," he said. "Just wow."

• • •

The party was held at the founder's home on Walker Lane. It was only twenty minutes from my apartment but a world away.

The house was a mansion. Or, more accurately, a villa, since it was Italian in design with rock and stucco exterior, a large, pillared portico, and beautiful wrought-iron front doors. Gas lights highlighted the brick-lined arched portals of the four-car garage. The yard was lit like a resort with lush landscaping and statuary.

Nicholas took my arm, and we walked up to the front door. A man standing in the lit portico opened the door for us. As we stepped inside the foyer we were embraced by a rush of light, smells, and music. The floor was polished wood, covered in places with lush area rugs. A brass chandelier, at least eight feet in diameter, hung above us from the high, domed ceiling.

In the sitting room across from the front door, a young woman was playing a harp next to a group I assumed, from the instruments around them, were members of a string quartet taking a break. I had never been inside such a luxurious home. I felt even more out of place than I had at La Caille. As usual, Nicholas was in his element.

"I don't think they'll be serving jalapeño poppers and Budweiser," I said.

"And the party will be the worse for it," he replied.

"May I take your coat?" a young man asked.

"Yes, please," Nicholas said. He helped me off with the stole Zoey had also brought me and handed it to the man.

Just then a mature, silver-haired man wearing a beautiful burgundy suit walked up to us. He was accompanied by an elegant woman I guessed to be his wife. "Nicholas," he said. "You made it."

"And this time you brought someone," the woman said. "And she's lovely."

"Thank you," I said.

"Elise, this is Alan McKay, our senior partner, and his better half, Careen."

"Thank you for having us," I said. "Your home is beautiful."

"Thank you, dear. We enjoy it."

"Food and drink is that way," Alan said, pointing to a side room. "Please, enjoy yourselves."

"Thanks, Alan," Nicholas said. "Careen."

Our hosts flitted away like butterflies.

"They were nice," I said.

"They're good people," Nicholas said. "Alan is the firm's founder and senior partner. He's also the one who brought me over from the prosecutor's office."

The party was considerably smaller than the one at La Caille, with maybe thirty guests in all. As we walked around I recognized some of the lawyers from a couple weeks earlier.

"Will Scott and Sharon be here?" I asked.

"No. Scott's not a partner. At least not yet."

"How many partners are there?"

"Eleven."

"And how many lawyers does your firm have?"

"Ninety-seven."

"How come you're the one with your name on the door?"

"They like me."

There were two food tables in the dining room, one savory, one sweet. At the head of the savory table was a man in a white chef's coat and hat, carving roast beef. There were also various hors d'oeuvres: bacon-wrapped scallops, crab puffs, jumbo prawns, caviar, carpaccio, and sushi.

The sweet table had three chocolate fountains with dark, white, and milk chocolates, the bases of the fountains surrounded by fruit. There were miniature key lime pies and cheesecakes, sweet croissants, puff pastries, baklava, millefoglie, and dipped chocolates.

"This is amazing," I said. "I think I'm going to gain weight."

"I'll help," Nicholas said.

We filled up our plates and sat down near the musicians. A few people came by to talk to Nicholas. They were all very warm and welcoming.

When I had finished my plate, Nicholas said, "Would you like to see the house?"

"I'd love to. Will they mind?"

"No," Nicholas said. "Alan loves to show it off."

"Why wouldn't he?" I said.

Nicholas led me up the circular stairs to a long hallway, both sides of which were lined with doors. The hallway led to another hallway and ended at a loft and another set of stairs.

"I could get lost in here," I said.

"Lots of people do," he said. "Come look at this." We walked into a spacious room lined with bookshelves, many filled with leather books. It had a fireplace with an antique model of a ship on its mantel, and in the center of the room was a beautiful antique desk. The ceiling was high and multifaceted with a wooden beam stretching the length of the room.

"This is Alan's den," Nicholas said.

"It's beautiful."

"Alan likes nice things."

I turned back to him. "Are Alan and Careen happy?"

Nicholas pondered the question. "They've been married almost forty years, so I hope so. Alan's not an especially affectionate man, so their relationship is very partner-like, which isn't necessarily a bad thing."

"But he's not cheating on her."

Nicholas shook his head. "Oh no. He's a man of strong ethics and a very conservative Catholic.

He once told one of the lawyers, 'If you're going through a midlife crisis, don't cheat. Buy yourself a Ferrari instead. It's cheaper.' " Nicholas smiled. "Want to see something cool?"

"Yes."

He pushed on one of the shelves, and it opened into a room. I clapped. "That's like in the movies."

"Every man wants a bookshelf that opens into a secret room."

"Where does it go?"

"Come inside," he said.

We stepped into the room. Like the outer room it had bookshelves, though the books weren't legal tomes but novels and personal reading, including a few Grisham, Patterson, and Vince Flynn thrillers. There were also several framed photographs of Alan with famous people, including President Bill Clinton, Bob Hope, and Maureen O'Hara.

"Actually, it's a safe room," Nicholas said. "In case terrorists or someone crazy breaks into his house. They can hide in here until the police arrive."

"Sometimes I'd like a safe room to hide in," I said.

"To hide from what?" Nicholas asked.

"Life."

Nicholas looked at me, then nodded as if he understood. "My father served in Vietnam. When I was young he told me that everyone needs an emotional foxhole. A place to hide when life's storms hit."

"Do you?"

"Of course," he said. "There's a quote widely misattributed to Plato that says, 'Be kind, for everyone you meet is fighting a hard battle.' It's true. Everyone has struggles. Everyone has suffered more than you know. That includes you and me."

I didn't know what to say, so I just nodded.

We walked back downstairs. The string quartet had resumed playing. Nicholas introduced me to a few more people, and then we went back and sat down next to the musicians.

As I looked around the ornately furnished room, I wondered what Nicholas's house must be like. "Where do *you* live?" I asked.

"Not far from here, actually." He suddenly smiled. "Would you like to see my house?"

"Yes."

His smile turned to a conspicuous grin.

"What?" I asked.

"When I first offered the contract you asked if this ended up back at my place. I bet you didn't think you'd be asking me to go."

I grinned back. "A lot has changed since then," I said.

Nicholas lived less than ten minutes away. His home was new, a Cape Cod–style house with shutters and a large front porch. He pulled his car into the garage. The door from the garage opened into the kitchen, where he flipped on the lights. The room was bright and immaculate, with not even a dish in the sink.

"This is really cute," I said.

"Wasn't really going for *cute,*" he replied.

"It's big," I said.

"For one person it is."

"It's big for a lot of people," I said.

"Hopefully I won't always be living here alone," he replied.

There were pictures on the wall. "Is this your family?" I asked.

He nodded.

"This is you with the long hair?"

"I'm afraid so."

"How old were you?"

He leaned forward for a closer look. "I think I was fifteen in that one." In none of the pictures was Nicholas older than fifteen or sixteen.

"These are your parents?" I asked.

"Yes."

"Have they ever been here?"

"No. My mother died before I built the home. My father wouldn't come."

"You know, you might be the cleanest bachelor in the country. You must have a cleaner."

"Rosa," he said. "She comes once a week. But actually, I'm pretty OCD. I don't like a messy house."

"I would drive you crazy."

I looked over a long row of porcelain figurines he had displayed on a shelf. He had three female nudes with angel wings, a larger piece of a mother breast-feeding her baby, and a glossy figurine of Don Quixote sitting in a chair holding an open book on his lap and a sword in his hand. "Tell me about these," I said.

"I collect Lladró. I just think they're beautiful. There's one piece I'm coveting, but I haven't gotten up the nerve to buy it yet. It's Cinderella in her pumpkin carriage with her horses and groomsmen. It's more than thirty thousand dollars."

"Wow," I said. "I can't imagine spending that much on art. Do you think you'll buy it?"

"I'll buy it someday," he said.

"I hope you let me see it when you do."

"Of course. You like Cinderella?"

"Who doesn't like Cinderella?"

He just looked at me thoughtfully, then changed the subject. "So are you ready for New York?"

"I haven't finished packing, but I'm very excited." I looked at him. "May I ask you a delicate question?"

"Of course."

"Are we sharing a room in New York?"

For a moment he just looked at me, and I had no idea how he was taking the question. Had I embarrassed him by implying that I didn't want to be with him, or had I embarrassed myself by presuming that he would? "I'm sorry," I said. "I didn't know."

"No, we're not," he said. "I booked you a separate room. It's in the contract." The moment settled into silence. Then he said, "It's late. I better get you home."

We were mostly quiet on the drive back to my apartment. He pulled up front and walked me to my door.

"Thank you for coming with me tonight," he said. "I've never enjoyed the partners' party more."

"Best partners' party I've ever been to," I said, smiling. "Thank you for letting me into your world."

We just stood there looking at each other. I suppose that I was still afraid I had offended him with my question about rooms in New York. But even greater than my fear was my desire that he would kiss me—not just on the cheek as he did in public, but really kiss me, passionately. Finally he leaned forward and kissed me on the cheek. "Good night, Elise."

"Good night, Nicholas," I said softly, hiding my disappointment. "I'll see you Monday morning."

He turned and walked away. I walked alone into my dark apartment. *The night had been magical. Why didn't he kiss me? Was I reading this all wrong?*

# Chapter Twenty-three

*I'm a long way from Montezuma Creek.*

## ELISE DUTTON'S DIARY

Monday morning, Nicholas arrived at my apartment a little after eight-thirty. I came to the door dragging my suitcase, which he looked at in wonder. "That's what you're bringing?"

"Yes."

"Did I tell you we'd be gone for five days or five weeks?"

"A woman needs more things."

"Playing the gender card," he said, smiling. "Let me get that." He lugged my massive bag down the stairs, opened his car trunk by remote, and dropped it inside while I climbed into the passenger seat.

He turned to me and said, "Ready for an adventure?"

"I'm always ready for an adventure," I said.

On the way to the airport Nicholas asked, "When was the last time you flew?"

"It's been a while."

"How long's a while?"

"About eleven years. It was my honeymoon."

"Where did you go?"

"Orange County. We went to Disneyland."

The airport was thick with travelers. I didn't know if it was busier than usual since I hadn't flown for so long.

"I can't believe all the people," I said. "Is it always this crowded?"

"It's the season. The airports are always crazy during the holidays." He looked at me. "Are you afraid of flying?"

"No," I said, shaking my head. "I'm afraid of . . . *not* flying."

"What do you mean?"

"As long as you're in the air there's no problem, right? It's coming back to earth that's the problem."

He grinned. "I think you just said something profound about life."

Our flight was direct from Salt Lake to JFK. Nicholas had booked two first-class tickets, which secretly thrilled me. I had never flown first-class before. We boarded first, before the throng of passengers that surrounded the gate.

"So this is how the other half lives," I said, sitting back in the wide, padded seat.

"When you fly as much as I do, it's more of a necessity than a luxury."

"It's still luxury," I said.

I must have looked a little nervous as the plane took off because he reached over and took my hand. Or maybe he just wanted to hold my hand. I hoped for the latter.

"Is our hotel in the city?" I asked.

"We're staying at the Parker Meridien on Fifty-Sixth," he said. "It's a nice hotel. French. And it's close to things. It's only six blocks from Rockefeller Center."

"That's where the big Christmas tree is," I said.

He nodded. "And we're only one block from Fifth Avenue."

"What's on Fifth Avenue?"

"Shopping," he said.

The flight was just a little over four hours. Nicholas fell asleep shortly after they served us lunch. As hard as he worked, I wasn't surprised. Even though I hadn't slept well the night before, I couldn't sleep on the plane. I was too excited. I felt like a girl on her first school field trip. Nicholas didn't wake until we began our descent. He rubbed his eyes, looked around, then checked his watch. "I slept for two hours. Why didn't you wake me?"

"You needed the sleep," I said.

After we had disembarked, Nicholas stopped in a terminal store for some melatonin, then I followed him through the labyrinth of JFK to get our luggage. Downstairs, next to the baggage carousel, was a man in a black suit and cap holding a sign with my name on it.

## ELISE DUTTON

"Is that for me?" I asked, which I realized was a foolish question.

"Of course," Nicholas said.

"I've never had someone holding a sign for me."

The man took our bags, and we followed him out into the cold to a black Lincoln Town Car. The ride took us across the Triborough Bridge into Manhattan, which gave us a clear view of the city's famous skyline. "Is that the Empire State Building?" I asked, pointing at a tall building lit red and green.

Nicholas nodded. "They light it for the season. The last time I was here it was purple to honor our soldiers with the Purple Heart."

The Parker Meridien was just off Sixth Avenue. The lobby was spacious with modern European design and a wry sense of humor. The elevators had televisions that played old Charlie Chaplin movies or Tom and Jerry cartoons, and the room's Do Not Disturb sign was a long hanger that read FUGGETABOUTIT, congruent with the hotel's slogan, "Uptown. Not Uptight."

After Nicholas checked us in, a bellman brought our bags to our rooms on the eleventh floor, just two doors from each other.

For dinner we ate Thai food at a tiny restaurant near the hotel. We said goodnight to each other outside my hotel room.

"I need to do some prep work for tomorrow," Nicholas said. "So I'll see you in the morning. My meetings begin at nine. If you'd like to have breakfast together, there's Norma's on the main floor. Or, you can sleep in and order room service. Whatever you want."

"I want to be with you," I said.

He looked pleased with my reply. "I'll knock on your door at seven-forty-five. Don't forget to turn your watch ahead two hours. I'll see you in the morning." He kissed me on the cheek.

He started to go, but I stopped him. "Nicholas."

"Yes?"

"Thank you."

"You're welcome, Elise. Sleep tight."

I shut my door and lay down on top of the bed thinking about how happy I was. I had never had so much fun.

There was only one week left on our contract.


I didn't fall asleep until after two, so I was tired when Nicholas knocked on my door at a quarter to eight. He looked sharp in his suit and tie.

"You look nice," I said. "Very professional." I didn't. I had just pulled on some jeans and a sweater.

"Shall we go?"

189

Norma's was a hip restaurant located in the hotel's lobby. I looked over the orange and black menu. "So many choices. Everything looks good."

"They're famous for their breakfasts."

"Oh my," I said, laughing. "Look at this. The Zillion Dollar Lobster Frittata. It's a thousand dollars."

"That's with ten ounces of sevruga caviar," he said. "Read what it says underneath the price."

"Norma dares you to expense this." I looked up. "What would you do if I ordered that?"

"Cancel tonight's dinner."

"I'll get something else," I said quickly. "Who are you meeting with this morning?"

"It's a software company called Revelar. They're buying up a competitor, and I'm here to make sure that they cross their *t*'s and dot their *i*'s. What are you going to do today?"

"I'm not sure yet."

"Well, unfortunately, it's New York, so there's not much to do," he said. "Especially at Christmastime."

I grinned. "I thought I'd walk around and see the sights."

"You could take the ferry to the Statue of Liberty and Ellis Island. Or you could take a tour of the Empire State Building. Also, you're not far from Fifth Avenue, where all the good shopping is—Saks, Tiffany's, Cartier, Prada, the good stuff."

"The good expensive stuff," I said.

"I'll be done a little after four. I made reservations for six at Keens Steakhouse. Then I thought we'd take in a show."

"What are we going to see?"

"That's a surprise," he said. He looked down at his watch. "I better go." He downed his coffee, then stood. "I'll see you this afternoon."

"Good luck," I said.

He stopped and turned back. "I almost forgot." He handed me his credit card. "Have fun."

I just looked at it. "What am I supposed to do with it?"

"Use it."

I watched him walk out. Then I put the card in my pocket and ordered another cup of hot chocolate.

I went back to my room to finish getting ready, then I took a taxi down to the Empire State Building and rode the elevator one hundred two floors to the top observation deck. It was amazing to look out over the entire city. Afterward I walked just a few blocks over to Macy's on Thirty-Fourth Street, joining the throngs of sightseers gathered in front of the store to see the famous animated holiday windows. The theme was the Magic of Christmas, which seemed appropriate for me this year.

I got into a taxi to go back to the hotel but, on a

191

whim, asked the driver for a recommendation for a good place to eat lunch. He was from São Paulo and he took me to a café in Little Brazil just a block off Sixth Avenue. The stew my waiter recommended was different but good. To drink I had a sugarcane juice mixed with pineapple juice. I walked the ten blocks back to the hotel, undressed, and took a nap. I woke to my room phone ringing.

"I'm sorry I'm late," Nicholas said. "Our meetings went long."

"What time is it?" I asked, sitting up.

"Did I wake you?"

"Yes."

"It's almost five. We should leave for dinner in a half hour."

"I'll be ready," I yawned. I got out of bed, splashed water on my face, dressed in a nicer outfit, and fixed my hair. I was putting on fresh makeup when he knocked. I opened the door. He was still wearing his suit but with a fresh shirt and his collar open. He looked handsome. He always looked handsome.

Keens Steakhouse was in the Garment District between Fifth and Sixth Avenues, though, at the time of its founding, in 1885, the area was considered the Theater District and was frequented by those on both sides of the curtain.

The restaurant was crowded, and the inside

was paneled in dark mahogany, covered with framed black-and-white pictures. The rooms were mostly lit by indirect lighting, creating the ambience of a nineteenth-century gentlemen's club, which, in fact, it was. The tables were close together and skirted with white linen cloths. A large, gilt-framed picture of a nude hung above the bar, reminding me of an old western saloon.

Nicholas ordered a half dozen oysters on the shell, which I tried but didn't care for. Then I had tomatoes and onions with blue Stilton cheese, and we shared a Chateaubriand steak for two. The food was incredible.

"What's that on the ceiling?" I asked.

He looked up. "Pipes."

"Pipes?"

"Clay smoking pipes. Every one of them is numbered. In the old days you would request your pipe, and they would find it by its number and bring it to your table. I'm not sure how many pipes are still up there, but I've heard more than eighty thousand. They belonged to people like Teddy Roosevelt, Babe Ruth, Albert Einstein, Buffalo Bill Cody, pretty much everybody who was famous came here. Except the women. It used to be that women weren't allowed inside. It took a lawsuit from King Edward the Seventh's paramour to open it to women."

"When was that?"

"Turn of the century."

"Just a decade ago?"

He smiled. "No. The previous century."

Our conversation was interrupted by my cell phone ringing. "Sorry, I forgot to turn it off," I said. I glanced at the screen, then quickly pressed the power button.

"Was it important?"

"No. It was Dan."

"Does he call you often?"

"No. More lately since his wife left him."

"His wife," Nicholas said. "The one that was your friend?"

I nodded. "Kayla."

"And he wants a shoulder to cry on?"

"He wants more than a shoulder. He wants to get back together."

"He told you that?"

"Right after he reminded me that it was my fault he divorced me."

"Your fault?"

I nodded. "Because of—" I caught myself. "It doesn't matter," I said. "There's no way I would ever go back to him."

"Did you tell him that?"

"Yes."

Nicholas nodded. "Good," he said. "You deserve better than him. So what did you do today?"

"I went to the top of the Empire State Building. Then I walked over to Macy's and looked at their windows, then I went to a café in Little Brazil for lunch and had this interesting stew. I don't remember what it's called, but the waiter said it's the Brazilian national dish."

"It's called *feijoada*," Nicholas said.

I looked at him in amazement. "Is there anything you don't know?"

He shook his head. "I don't know."

I laughed. "You are the smartest person I know."

"Then you must not know many people," he replied.

As we were finishing dessert, he reached into his pocket and brought out a piece of paper. "I have something for you. I should have done this for you earlier."

"What is it?"

"During my meetings I made a list of things you should do or where you should eat during the day. Actually, it's mostly eating."

I reviewed the list.

Serendipity 3 (frozen hot chocolate)
Hamburger in lobby at
Parker Meridien
Met Museum
Ellen's Stardust Diner (breakfast)
Carnegie Deli (egg cream)

"All right," I said looking up, "give me the rundown."

"Serendipity 3 is between Second and Third Avenues. It's famous for celebrity clients like Marilyn Monroe and Andy Warhol, but food-wise, it's famous for the frozen hot chocolate. On their fiftieth anniversary they created the world's most expensive dessert, which was basically a thousand-dollar ice cream sundae."

"A thousand dollars. What's on it, gold?"

"That's exactly what's on it. Twenty-three-karat gold leaf, Madagascar vanilla, the world's most expensive chocolate, and gold caviar."

"I won't be having that."

"Thank you," he said. "Next on the list, if you're craving a burger, the hamburger joint in the lobby of our hotel has one of New York's best."

"There's a hamburger joint in our hotel?"

"I know, strange, right? It's behind the curtain just past the registration counter. You wouldn't know it's there unless someone told you. The menu signs are all handwritten in marker." He looked back down at the list. "Next is the Met, the Metropolitan Museum of Art. But I'm sure you're already familiar with it."

"We send students there."

"Time to send yourself," he said. "Be warned: it will take most of your day. And for breakfast, if you want something different, we're not far from Ellen's Stardust Diner. It's a retro fifties diner that attracts a lot of Broadway actor wannabes as waiters and waitresses, so occasionally they break into song. The challah French toast is especially good.

"Then, just a couple blocks from the hotel is the Carnegie Deli. It's also a good lunch stop. They're known for their pastrami and corned beef, but I'd go there just for the egg cream."

"What's an egg cream?"

"It's a soda, basically. Ironically it has neither eggs nor cream, but you must try it. I always have at least one when I come here. The Reuben sandwiches are definitely more than you can eat at one sitting."

"There's so much to do here," I said.

"So much to eat," he said. He glanced down at his watch. "We better get going."

"Where are we going?"

"Radio City Music Hall."

The cab dropped us off a half block away from Radio City. The sign on the marquee read:

### The Radio City Christmas Spectacular
### Featuring the Rockettes

We picked up our tickets and found our seats in the fifth row of the middle section. The room buzzed with excitement. Nicholas leaned into me. "I think you'll like this."

"Have you seen it before?"

"No. But I've heard good things about it. Everyone needs to see the Rockettes at least once in their lifetime."

"When I think of the Rockettes, I just think of legs," I said.

He laughed. "Well, that's what they're famous for. And dancing."

There were fourteen musical numbers, concluding with a living nativity, the Wise Men arriving at the manger on a caravan of real camels. The showstopper was the fifth act, "The Parade of the Wooden Soldiers," when, in the finale, a cannon shot knocked the dancers over like a line of dominoes. As the curtain fell, the crowd joined in singing "Joy to the World."

The temperature outside had dropped to well below freezing, and Nicholas pulled me in close as we walked back to our hotel. I only wished that it was farther away.

# Chapter Twenty-four

*I bought Nicholas a present today.
Even though it emptied my savings
account, it's nothing compared to
what he's spent on me. I hope he
appreciates the widow's mite.*

## ELISE DUTTON'S DIARY

I slept in the next morning. Nicholas had a breakfast meeting with his client, so he left without waking me. He also said that I needed the rest, which was true. He had left a note under my door asking if I would do him a favor and pick up something for him at Tiffany on Fifth Avenue. I had already planned on shopping. I wanted to get something for Nicholas.

I ordered room service, which was another first for me, then sat in a robe near the window looking out over the city while I ate my oatmeal brûlée. I felt a long way from Montezuma Creek.

After breakfast, I took a cab to the Metropolitan Museum. Since I had started working at ICE I had purchased more than a thousand tickets for the museum, but I had never been there myself. I went into the sales office and met my sales representative, Justin, who was demonstrably excited to meet me after all these years. He was young, flamboyant, chubby, and bald and looked nothing like I expected.

He insisted on taking me on a personal tour of the museum's highlights. The breadth of the collection was stunning. I was amazed to see actual Picassos and Rembrandts, and Van Gogh's sunflowers.

Around two o'clock I thanked Justin and took a cab to the Montblanc store on Madison Avenue. As I looked over a display case of pens, one of the sales personnel approached me. "May I help you?"

"Hi," I said. "I need to buy a gift for a friend. A pen."

"Male or female?" he asked.

"Male. And he's a lawyer."

He smiled a little at my description. "I'm certain I can find you something that will impress him. How much were you thinking of spending?"

I swallowed. Many of the pens were in excess of a thousand dollars. I lightly grimaced. "About five hundred dollars."

The man just nodded. "We'll find him a pen he'll never forget."

Even though the price of the pen was just a fraction of what Nicholas had spent on me, it was nearly all my savings. But it was something I wanted to do for him. It wasn't the amount of money he'd spent on me as much as it was the way he'd done it. Lovingly. He had shown me more love than my own husband and my own father ever had. In our pretend affair, he had opened my eyes to what a real relationship could and should be.

"I recommend this one," the man said, delicately presenting me a pen. "We just got it in. This is our Bohème Marron pen. The rollerball is a bit more practical than the fountain pen, and better priced."

"It's pretty," I said. "Is that a gem?"

"Yes. It's a brown topaz."

"How much is it?"

"It's five hundred and twenty-five dollars, plus tax."

"Okay," I said. "I read that you can engrave something on it."

"Yes, ma'am."

"How long does that take?"

"It usually takes a day or two."

"Is it possible to do it any sooner? I was hoping to give it to him this evening."

He smiled at me. "If you can come back in an hour, I'll walk it over to the engraver myself. What would you like engraved on it?"

I thought for a moment, then said, "Love, Elise."

"Let me get an order form." He wrote down

my words, then showed it to me for approval and a signature. I gave him my credit card. "Very well, Ms. Elise, I will have this for you in one hour."

"Thank you."

I left Montblanc and walked a block to the famous Tiffany store. I went up to the first sales counter I saw. "I'm here to pick something up for a friend of mine."

"Were you thinking gold, silver, or diamonds?" she asked.

"I'm sorry, I meant, he already purchased the item. He wanted me to pick it up for him."

"My mistake," she said kindly. "What name would that be under?"

"Nicholas Derr," I said.

"Nicholas Derr," she repeated. "Just a moment." She typed something into her computer, then walked away from the counter, returning about five minutes later. "Mr. Derr requested that the gift remain wrapped," she said.

"That's fine."

"I will need to see some ID."

"Of course." I brought out my wallet. "There's my license."

She looked at it. "Elise Dutton." She looked at the receipt on the box. "Elise Dutton. Very good." She handed me back my license, then the box. "Let me get you a bag for that." She lifted the famous robin's egg blue bag and set the box inside. "Thank you for visiting us."

I walked back to the Montblanc store and picked up the pen, then walked the four blocks back to the hotel. My feet were getting sore from all my walking. My phone rang on the way. I was excited to talk to Nicholas but disappointed when I saw it was Dan calling.

"What do you want, Dan?"

"We need to talk, Elise."

"No we don't."

"I've discovered some things about your new *friend*. So open your door."

"I'm not home."

Don't lie to me. I can see your car."

"I'm not home, Dan. I'm in New York."

He paused. "What are you doing in New York?"

"Living," I said. I hung up on him. He called back, but I didn't answer. Then he texted me.

**We need to talk about your lawyer "friend." Crucial**

I shook my head. There wasn't a thing he could tell me that I would consider crucial. Still, his text did make me curious. What could Dan possibly know about Nicholas? Then my phone rang again. I was going to tell Dan to stop calling when I saw it was Nicholas.

"Hi," I said.

"Hi. Are you at the hotel?"

"Not yet. I'm just walking back."

"How was your day?"

"Amazing."

"Good. We have dinner reservations at six. We should leave a half hour before."

"I'll be ready," I said. "What are we having for dinner?"

"How does Italian sound?"

"I love Italian."

"You'll love this place," he said. "See you in a few minutes."

Nicholas knocked on my door at five-thirty. He smiled when I opened. "Hi."

"How was your day?" I asked.

"Challenging. But let's not talk about it."

"Let me grab my coat," I said. "Just a minute."

He held the door open. "Did you get a chance to run by Tiffany's?" he asked.

"Yes. Let me grab that for you." I put on my coat, secretly put the Montblanc box in my purse, then brought over the Tiffany bag. "Here you go."

"Thanks for picking that up for me."

"No problem."

"I better leave it in my room," he said. "I'll be right back." He walked to his room, then returned empty-handed. "Shall we go?"

We had to wait awhile for a cab, and we arrived a few minutes late for our dinner reservation. The restaurant Nicholas had decided on was called Babbo, and it had a famous chef, Mario

Batali, who was sometimes on television. The atmosphere was elegant with, incongruently, loud rock music.

Everything was exquisite. I ordered wine with my meal. Babbo had more than two thousand wines, which they served *quartino*, meaning in a carafe that held about a glass and a half. Our waiter recommended a Calabrian wine called Cirò. Nicholas ordered sparkling water. After the waiter left, I asked, "Do you drink?"

He shook his head and said, "No," but nothing more.

The evening passed quietly between us, but not uncomfortably. Nicholas just seemed a little lost in thought, something I attributed to his "challenging" day.

As we were finishing our meals, Nicholas said, "Did you recognize who's sitting behind me?"

I looked over his shoulder. "Is that really Kevin Bacon?"

He nodded. "And his wife, Kyra Sedgwick." Just then someone walked over to their table to ask them for their autographs. They politely demurred.

"That's one of the things about New York," Nicholas said. "It's a cultural mecca."

"Like Montezuma Creek," I said.

Nicholas laughed. "Just like Montezuma Creek. After all, you did get the Harlem Globetrotters."

"Yes we did. That's my brush with fame."

"Now you can say you've been one degree from Kevin Bacon. Did you enjoy your meal?"

"Immensely. I don't think I'll ever be able to eat store-bought spaghetti sauce again."

"Then I've done you a service," he said. "One can get to be a food snob in New York."

"What was that last dish you had?"

"Lamb's brain Francobolli."

I just looked at him. "I can't tell if you're kidding me or not."

He smiled. "I'm not. They're famous for some interesting fare. But there was a reason I chose this place besides the food."

"And what was that?"

"Just a moment," he said. He stood up and left the table. He returned a couple minutes later and sat down. "I have something for you." He brought from his pocket the Tiffany box I had picked up earlier and set it in front of me.

"That was for me?"

"Of course."

I took the beautiful blue box, untied its ribbon, and lifted the lid. Inside was a velvet jewelry box. "What did you do?" I asked.

"Keep going," he said.

I set the cardboard box down on the table, then pried opened the jewelry box's lid. Inside was an exquisite rose gold pendant. It was conical, about an inch long, with elegant spiraled lines. I gasped.

"Do you like it?"

I looked up at him. "It's beautiful."

"It's from Paloma Picasso's collection," he said. "It was inspired by the hanging lanterns of Venice. That's why I thought it was appropriate we had Italian for dinner."

"This is too much."

"I know," he said. "Try it on."

I lifted the pendant from the box. "Would you help me put it on?"

"I'd love to," he said. He stood and walked around the table. I lifted the back of my hair as he draped the chain around my neck. The pendant fell to the top of my cleavage.

"I've never had anything so nice before," I said.

"Then it's about time," he said. I stood up and hugged him. "Thank you."

"I'm glad you like it."

"I don't like it, I love it."

We finished our desserts, olive oil and rosemary cake with a pistachio gelato, then we took a cab to Rockefeller Center to see the tree. Even though it was cold enough to see our breaths, I left my coat open to reveal my new necklace.

The eighty-foot tree was brilliantly lit, and the plaza was crowded with tourists. Beneath the statue of Prometheus, skaters glided gracefully, and some not so gracefully, across the rink.

We had been there for a while when I said, "I have something for you too."

Nicholas looked at me in surprise. "You do?"

"Remember when we signed the contract, I asked you if you had a pen? You said, 'I'm a lawyer. That's like asking me if I have a lung.' "

He grinned. "And you made a snarky remark about me not having a heart."

"I was wrong," I said. "You're all heart." I took the pen from my purse and handed it to him.

"What's this?"

"It's a present."

He unwrapped the box. "You bought me a Montblanc pen." He looked up at me. "Elise, this is way too expensive."

"It's nothing compared to what you've spent on me."

"You can't . . ."

I touched his lips. "Remember when you got mad at me for complaining you spend too much? Now I'm telling you the same thing. I know it's not much in your world, but it's all I have. Please let me enjoy this."

He just stood there quietly as the world noisily swirled around us. He looked deeply affected. "Thank you."

"I just wanted to give you something that you would use. And maybe when you saw it, you would think of me. And remember this time we've had together."

"I don't need a pen for that," he said softly.

"Thank you for bringing me to New York. Thank

you for everything you've done this season. I don't know why you've done all this, but thank you."

"You still don't know why?"

I dared not say what I hoped, that he felt about me the way I did about him. That he loved me. We gazed into each other's eyes, then he put his hand behind my head and gently pulled me into him and we kissed. Then we kissed and kissed. It was the first time I'd kissed anyone in years, but I'd never kissed anyone like that in my entire life. I had never felt more swept away, more lost in someone else, or even my own head. When we parted I said breathlessly, "So much for the platonic clause."

"Men can't have platonic relationships."

We kissed again. In spite of my best efforts, I'd done exactly what I knew I shouldn't. I'd fallen deeply in love with a man who was going to leave me.

We walked back to the hotel holding hands. We stopped outside my room and kissed again.

"Do you want to come inside?" I asked.

"Desperately," he said. He breathed out slowly. "But I better not."

"You're right," I said. "Are you sure?"

"Barely," he replied. We kissed some more, and then I reluctantly pulled back a little, just until our lips were apart, our noses still touching. "I better let you get some sleep."

"Okay."

"Thank you for tonight. For everything. I love my necklace."

"I love *you,*" he said.

The words shocked me. I pulled back and looked at him. As much as I had wanted to hear those words, I hadn't expected to. Emotion welled up inside me. Of course I loved him, but he couldn't love me.

"What's wrong?" he said.

I couldn't speak. I kissed him again, then quickly ducked inside my room, leaving him standing there in the hallway, confused. I fell on my bed and cried. I also felt confused, torn by two equally powerful emotions, joy for being loved and fear of being loved, horrified by the truth that he'd fallen in love with someone he didn't really know and wouldn't love once he did.

# Chapter Twenty-five

*It's been said that "perfect love
casts out all fear," but, in my case,
it seems to be the source of it.*

### ELISE DUTTON'S DIARY

I woke the next morning crying. I had had a terrible nightmare. Nicholas and I had gotten married. I was in an elegant, beaded ivory wedding dress, he was in tails with a wingtip shirt and red band tie and sash. We ran from the church to a car decorated by our guests, climbed inside, and drove off. Then Nicholas looked in the mirror. "What's that?"

"What's what, dear?" I asked.

"In the backseat. There's a box or something." We both turned around. In the backseat was my daughter's coffin.

I looked in the mirror at my necklace. It was the most beautiful piece of jewelry I had ever owned. Even my wedding ring paled in comparison. But

I couldn't keep it. Just like I couldn't keep him.

Nicholas called my room three times the next morning. I didn't answer. I was too afraid. Then he called my cell phone, which I didn't answer either. Finally he knocked on my door. "Elise," he asked through the door. "Are you all right?"

*I should have answered the phone,* I thought. Now he was going to see me, puffy eyes and all.

"Elise, are you all right?"

I opened the door just enough to see him. "I'm sorry," I said. "I'm okay."

He looked at me anxiously. "What's wrong?"

"It's nothing," I said.

He looked baffled. "Nothing?"

"We can talk later," I said. "After your meetings."

He looked at me for a moment more, then said, "I meant what I said last night. I do love you."

My eyes welled up. "I know."

"I'll be back soon. We'll talk. Everything will be all right."

"Okay," I said.

He walked off down the hall. I went back to bed, but couldn't get back to sleep. After an hour I dressed and went out. I wandered around Central Park. I tried to calm myself, to believe his words that everything would be okay, but the fear didn't leave. It had been with me for so long it didn't take eviction lightly.

Before you judge me too harshly, consider your own deepest fears—real or imagined. Actually, all fear is born of the imagination, which means that the danger we fear doesn't need be rational or even real to be potent. Like my fear of snakes.

When I was eighteen I drove my car off the highway into a ditch because there was a snake on the road. It didn't matter that the snake couldn't have bitten me through the car. It didn't matter that the snake probably wasn't even poisonous or might even have already been dead. It didn't even matter that swerving off the road at fifty miles per hour posed a much greater danger than the snake I was frightened of. Fear doesn't listen to reason. It takes its own counsel.

While my saner self recognized that my fear of snakes was partially irrational, my fear of rejection wasn't. I'd never been bitten by a snake, but I'd been bitten by rejection more times than I could remember. After all the attacks and abandonment I'd endured since Hannah's death, my heart wasn't about to believe that someone might be different. Not even someone as beautiful as Nicholas.

Nicholas came back to the hotel at four, and we went to dinner at a restaurant close by, the Redeye Grill. We started with small talk, which considering where we'd ended the evening before seemed especially peculiar. He waited until we had mostly eaten before he asked, "Elise, what's wrong?"

I didn't answer. I was afraid to answer.

"Was it because I told you that I love you?"

I slowly nodded.

He frowned deeply. "And you don't love me."

"I'm madly in love with you," I said.

His look of sadness gave way to a smile. "Then what's the problem?"

"You can't really love me," I said. "You don't know me."

"I know you," he said. "I know that in spite of a harsh childhood you're kind and giving and sweet. I know that you give more than you take. I know that you're grateful for even the smallest acts of kindness. And I know that I can't live without you. What more do I need to know?"

My eyes welled up with pain. I could no longer keep my secret from him. "There's something you don't know about me. Something I've done. Something horrible."

He looked at me for a moment, then said, "Does it have to do with Hannah?"

# Chapter Twenty-six

*I had locked from him the deepest chambers of my fear, only to discover that he had his own key.*

## Elise Dutton's Diary

Every part of me froze. When I could speak I asked, "How do you know about Hannah?"

He didn't answer. I could see my fear reflected in his eyes. I would say that I felt as if I'd been stripped naked, but it was more than that. I felt as if my skin had been flayed, my innermost parts exposed to the world.

"How long have you known this?" I asked. "Did you know before the contract?"

He gazed at me anxiously, then said softly, "I knew long before the contract."

"How?"

He looked down for a moment, then said, "We've met before."

"I've never met you before."

"Yes, we have," he said. "But in the state you

were in, I doubt you would remember. I wouldn't have." After a pause he said, "Do you remember that I told you I worked for the prosecutor's office?" He paused again, and I was terrified of what he was going to say. "I had been there about a year when we got a call from the Salt Lake County Sheriff's Office saying a child had been left in a car and died of hyperthermia. They weren't sure whether to arrest the mother. I was sent out to assess the situation."

Suddenly I knew who he was. Tears welled up in my eyes. "You're the man who interviewed me."

He nodded.

I was speechless.

"I knew it was an accident the moment I saw you. And that no punishment the justice system could dish out would be as bad as what you were already experiencing. I went back and convinced them not to prosecute."

His words rushed through me, freezing me like ice. No, broken ice. I felt shattered and pierced.

"You knew the whole time."

He warily gazed into my eyes, then slowly nodded.

"Have you been stalking me for all these years?"

"Of course not. A couple of months ago I saw you in the elevator. I knew I recognized you, I just didn't remember from where. After I got out I remembered."

For several minutes I was speechless. I had never felt so exposed before. "Why did you lie to me?"

"I didn't lie to you."

"You withheld the truth. That's the same as a lie."

"It wasn't important."

I stared at him incredulously. "It wasn't important?"

"No," he said.

"It was to me," I said. "How could you be so cruel?"

He looked stunned. "Elise . . ."

"I need to go," I said.

"Elise, please."

"I need to go," I repeated. "Now."

"All right. We'll go."

"Alone," I said.

He looked at me for a moment, then nodded. "All right."

I retrieved my coat from the coat check and walked alone back to the hotel.

# Chapter Twenty-seven

*It's been said that the truth will set you free. But the truth can also bury you. It's not the hurricane that breaks your heart, it's the phone call afterward informing you that all is lost.*

ELISE DUTTON'S DIARY

The night passed in a strange delirium. Nothing was what I thought it was. My Nicholas, my beautiful, safe fantasy man, was an intricate part of my worst nightmare. He was part of my past, and, whether he had intended to or not, he had reengulfed me in it.

The next morning Nicholas called me several times, but I didn't answer. The fourth time he left a message. "Elise, your flight to Salt Lake leaves at two-ten. It's nearly an hour ride to the airport, so you better leave the hotel by noon. I booked a car for you. It will be downstairs at the curb waiting for you at twelve. It will have a sign in the window with your name. If you have any problems, just ask the hotel attendant for help. Don't worry about checking out; I'll take care of everything.

"I won't be going with you. I'm going to stay here for an extra day so you can have time to think. I'm sorry for hurting you. I didn't mean to. I would never intentionally hurt you. I hope you can forgive me." Then he said something I didn't understand. "Please have faith in me. I understand your pain better than you know."

Hearing his voice intensified my emotion, and I felt like I might have some sort of breakdown. I sat on the floor of the shower crying for nearly an hour, the water pouring over me, mixing with my tears and carrying them to the drain.

I was two people, and it was tearing me apart. Part of me wanted to run to Nicholas for comfort. To be held and loved and protected by him. The other half wanted to deny ever knowing him and everything that had happened since the contract. Mostly, I just wanted to crawl back into the dark, safe cave of my previous world.

As I packed my bag, someone knocked on my door. My heart froze. I didn't want to see him, but I couldn't stop myself either.

I opened the door, but it was only a woman from housekeeping wanting to clean my room. I told her I'd be leaving shortly. A few minutes before twelve I dragged my bag out of the room. I stole a glance at Nicholas's door as if hiding the action from myself. I hoped he would be watching for me, but he wasn't.

The elevator door opened into the lobby, and I walked out to the street. A black town car was waiting at the curb with a sign that read DUTTON. The bellman put my bag in the trunk, and I cried as the car pulled away from the hotel.

"Are you okay, ma'am?" the driver asked.

I shook my head. "No."

He didn't say anything more.

My flight landed in Salt Lake a few minutes before five. I retrieved my bag, then took a cab back to my apartment. As I undressed I realized that I was still wearing the gold necklace Nicholas had given me. I poured myself a glass of wine and drank it. Then another. Then another. It had been a long time since I'd drunk to get drunk, but that's exactly what I was doing. Then I lay down on my bed and cried myself to sleep.

The next day was Saturday. I lay in bed until almost one in the afternoon. I was hungover and my head ached, but that was nothing compared to the pain I felt in losing Nicholas. I didn't have the energy or desire to get out of bed. Most of all I didn't have any reason to. I wondered if Nicholas had made it back to Salt Lake. I craved him. I missed him as much as I feared him. I hoped he would call, but he never did. I kept my phone nearby just in case it rang. It never did.

# Chapter Twenty-eight

*There is not only more to each soul's journey than we imagine, usually there is more than we* can *imagine.*

## ELISE DUTTON'S DIARY

My doorbell rang twice on Christmas Eve. Both times filled me with intense anticipation. The first time was the UPS man delivering a package from New York. It was from Nicholas. I supposed it was my last gift. I didn't open it. I couldn't bring myself to read his letter.

The second time the doorbell rang was later that afternoon. I was sure it was Nicholas. I hoped it was as much as I hoped it wasn't. I took a deep breath before looking through my door's peephole. Dan was standing outside leaning on one hand against my door. He must have known I was looking through the lens because he suddenly leaned forward and looked through the opposite side of the peephole until his eye filled my field of vision.

I pulled open the door. "What do you want?"

"Glad you finally decided to come home," he said.

"What do you want?" I repeated.

"I already told you what I want. I want us again. The way it should be."

"And I told you I wasn't interested."

"Why? Because you think you're in love?"

"No," I said. "It's over."

"So things didn't work out with the lawyer in New York."

I didn't answer.

"Well, it's for the better. With a past like his, you didn't want to get mixed up with that guy anyway."

"What are you talking about?" I said.

"Will you let me in? It's freezing out here."

I stepped back from the door, and he walked in. He sat on my sofa. "So, I got the lowdown on your lawyer. He's not who you think he is."

"No one ever is," I said.

"That's where you're wrong," Dan said. "I am. With me, what you see is what you get."

"You mean a narcissistic cheater," I said.

He grinned, looking more impressed by my words than insulted. "Looks like you've finally grown some attitude."

"It's about time I did."

"So let me tell you about your *friend*."

"I don't care," I said.

"Good. Because he's a first-class loser."

Hearing this made me angry. "No, he's nothing like you."

"Then you're not over him."

"He's a good man."

"Then you won't mind me telling you that he's a drunk."

I shook my head. "He doesn't even drink."

"Then maybe he stopped after he killed the family."

I looked at him. "What are you talking about?"

"Your friend has a serious criminal record. Or at least he should have one. He was driving drunk when he crashed his car into a family crossing a crosswalk. Two parents and two children. He killed three of them."

"You're a liar."

"I thought you might say that, so I brought proof. I printed it off the Internet."

He unfolded a piece of paper from his coat pocket and handed it to me. The headline read,

## For Three Deaths Teen Gets Two Years

Nicholas Derr, a 16-year-old Highland High School student, was sentenced to juvenile detention for up to two years after admitting Monday that he killed three and injured one in a DUI accident.

There were shouts of protest in 3rd

District Juvenile Court when Judge Anders handed down the sentence.

"He kills three people and he's out in just two years?" said Mark Buhler, a friend of the deceased family. "Where's the justice? Is that all their lives are worth?"

Derr had a blood-alcohol level at 0.10 percent; the Utah legal limit is 0.08. Derr and a friend (name withheld) were driving down 2100 south from a Parley's Canyon party where alcohol was being served when his vehicle struck the Hayes family in a crosswalk just north of Sugar House Park at 8:41 p.m. on December 7.

Vance Hayes (28), Michelle Hayes (27), and their two daughters, Olivia (3) and Victoria (1), were just leaving the park when witnesses say that Derr ran a red light and struck the family. The two young children were in a double stroller. Derr's car was estimated to be traveling nearly twice the speed limit of the 30 mph zone. The father and one-year-old were killed instantly. The mother was DOA at University of Utah Hospital. Only the three-year-old survived the crash. She sustained multiple broken bones and major internal injuries, but doctors believe she will recover. Derr and his friend were uninjured.

Derr, who had just received his driver's license two weeks before the accident, pleaded guilty to three counts of second-degree felony automobile homicide and one count of negligent injury. Derr has no previous DUIs or criminal record.

"He's a good kid," a neighbor, who asked to remain anonymous, said of Derr. "I've known him for years. He comes from a good family. He mows the lawn of one of the widows on our street and shovels her walk in the winter. One time some bullies were picking on my son and Nick protected him. I don't know what happened with this accident. He just made some bad choices, like any kid could."

Earlier this month, Judge Anders decided against ordering Derr to stand trial in adult court, where the teen would have faced up to 30 years at Utah State Prison. Derr will be eligible for parole in as few as twenty-four months.

I looked at the picture of an upside-down car and an area cordoned off with police tape. Then I looked up at Dan. His dark eyes brimmed with satisfaction. "Looks like the two of you have more in common than you thought."

"Get out of here," I said.

"Don't kill the messenger, honey."

"Get out of here!" I screamed.

He looked at me for a moment, then stood. "I should've figured. Two killers, no jail time. You're perfect for each other."

I slapped him so hard my hand stung. "Don't you ever call me that again!" I shouted. "Do you hear me? Never call me that again!"

Dan was stunned. The imprint of my hand was fresh on his cheek. "I've paid a thousand times over for my mistake. A thousand times a thousand. I have suffered and bled for something that I would give my life to have prevented. I would have gladly traded my life for hers, but I can't. But you will not hold this over my head anymore. I have paid the debt. Do you understand me?"

He didn't answer.

*"Do you understand me?"*

"Yes 'Lise."

"Now get out of here."

He slowly turned his back on me. He had just walked out the door when I shouted after him, "And you're right. Nicholas and I *are* perfect for each other." I slammed the door shut after him.

For the first time since the day Hannah died, I felt free. And I fully understood why Nicholas had been so good to me. He understood. He had weathered the same fierce storm.

I grabbed the package he'd sent and tore back the paper to reveal a satin box marked

WATERFORD CRYSTAL. I untied its ribbon and lifted the lid. Inside the red-velvet-lined box was a crystal Christmas ornament. A star. Next to the star was a scrolled parchment note tied with ribbon. I untied the ribbon and unrolled the note. It was written in Nicholas's hand.

My dear Elise,

It's been said that the Magi, wise men, gazed up into the night skies, following a star. But they were not looking for a star. They were looking for hope. Hope of a new world. Hope of redemption. Light is not found in dark places, and hope is not found looking down or looking back. May you always look up. It has been my greatest joy spending this holiday season with you. And though things did not end between us as I hoped, whatever the new year brings, I will always hope the best for you and be forever grateful for your love. I will always love you.

Nick

# Chapter Twenty-nine

*Our contract has expired.*

## Elise Dutton's Diary

When I arrived at Nicholas's home I knocked on his door, then rang his doorbell, but he didn't answer. There was one set of car tracks in the driveway, and I guessed he had gone somewhere. I sat down on the cold concrete porch to wait. The temperature dropped with the sun until it was well below freezing. Or at least until I was. I shivered with the cold, but I wasn't going to leave. I couldn't make myself leave.

It was after dark when Nicholas's car turned in to his driveway. His garage door opened, but he saw me and stopped before pulling in. He got out and walked up to me.

"What are you doing here?"

My chin was quivering with the cold, making it difficult to speak. "We had a date. Remember?"

He looked down a moment, then said, "That was before you said I was cruel and ran away."

My words pierced me. "I came to apologize."

For a moment he seemed unsure of what to say. "How long have you been waiting here?"

"Three hours."

"You must be freezing."

I nodded, my body involuntarily shuddering with the suggestion.

He put out his hand. "Come in and get warm."

He unlocked the front door, and we stepped into the foyer. His home was warm and dark, illuminated only by a hall light and the colorful blinking strands of his Christmas tree. He led me to a small den, told me to sit on the sofa, and then left the room. I could hear him moving around in the kitchen. It seemed that I sat there for the longest time before he returned without his coat and carrying a porcelain mug. "Drink this. It's hot cider."

"Thank you," I said, taking the cup from him with both hands. I sipped the hot drink while he sat down backward on the piano bench. The warm drink spread through my body. When I could speak I asked, "Do you play?"

He nodded. "Yes."

I didn't know what to say and I'm not sure he did either because the silence was interminable. He looked at me until I couldn't stand it anymore. Finally I took a deep breath and said, "Dan came by to see me this afternoon. He's still trying to get me back. He thought he could scare me away from you with this." I set the news-paper article on the table between us.

Nicholas barely glanced at it. "And he didn't even need it. I scared you away without it." He took a deep breath. "And you think I owe you an explanation?"

"You don't owe me anything," I said.

"Then why are you here?"

The question stung, filling my eyes with tears. I bowed my head, afraid to show my eyes, afraid to look into his. "After reading the article I realized that you really did understand me. And that you might be the only one in the world who could really love me."

He was silent for a moment, then said, "I'd like to explain what happened."

I looked up at him. "You don't have to."

"I want to," he said. "I was barely sixteen years old. I was a sophomore in high school. My girl-friend had broken up with me a couple days before. You know how teenagers are, all drama and hormones. I was depressed and had pretty much taken to my bed, just listening to music all night. A friend of mine came over to cheer me up. He talked me into going to a party some seniors were having up in the canyons.

"They had a keg. Everyone was drunk or getting there. I resisted, at first. My parents were Mormon, so we didn't have alcohol in our house. I had never even drunk alcohol before. But between the peer pressure and my depression and my friend nagging, I gave in. It was the worst mistake of my life. It didn't take much to get me drunk. I had maybe three beers. My friend was completely wasted, so I took his keys and drove us home."

I could see the pain grow in his eyes.

"We were coming down Parley's Canyon onto twenty-first south. I was driving fast, close to sixty miles per hour, when I reached Sugar House Park. Wrong place, wrong time. There was a young family leaving the park. They were in the crosswalk. A mom, dad, a three- and a one-year-old in a double stroller. It was dark, and I was driving so fast I don't know if I would have seen them anyway, but I hit them. The father saw me just before; he tried to push the stroller out of the way. He was killed instantly. I hit him and his wife and clipped the stroller, then rolled the car into a telephone pole.

"The mother was thrown more than eighty feet, but somehow she was still alive when the ambulance arrived. I climbed out of the car and walked around the scene like I was in a nightmare, listening to the mother scream for her children. When I have nightmares, that's what I hear, that mother's screams." He looked into my eyes. "The three-year-old lived. Her name is Olivia. She's seventeen now."

I let the story settle over me. When I could speak I asked, "Have you met her?"

"A year ago," he said softly. "I've taken flowers to the grave every year on the anniversary of their deaths."

"December seventh," I said. "That's where you were."

He nodded. "Last year I was in the cemetery, just kneeling there, praying for forgiveness, like I always do. When I stood, there was a teenage girl behind me. I hadn't heard her come up. She just looked at me for a moment and then she said, 'It's you, isn't it?'

"I said, 'I'm so sorry.' She looked at me for a moment and then she did something I'll never forget. She said, 'I forgive you.' " Nicholas's eyes welled up. "The power of those words. I fell back to my knees and wept. Olivia was almost the same age I was when I took her parents and sister from her. I don't know how she did it. But she knelt down next to me and held me. She said, 'You were just a kid, like me. Sometimes we do dumb things. Sometimes there are consequences.' " Nicholas shook his head. "I don't know how she found the strength to say that to the man who had killed her parents."

"What happened after the accident?" I asked.

"I was arrested. I was put in youth corrections for nineteen months—until my eighteenth birthday. It would have been longer—much longer—but because I was underage and it was my first offense, the judge ruled that I would be tried as an adolescent. A lot of people wanted me tried as an adult. Some of those people were waiting outside the juvie center with placards when I got out. They stood there and jeered at me. One called me a murderer. One had a drawing of a headstone with the word *justice*. I'll never forget a woman shaking a finger at me and saying, 'Rot in hell.' "

"I understand," I said.

He slowly nodded. "I know you do. You also understand that even though the law was done with me, my punishment had just begun. I carried the weight of what I'd done every day of my life. My relationship with my parents changed. My trial and fines had just about bankrupted them.

"My mother was severely depressed. She was very religious and she blamed herself for what had happened. She felt like God was punishing her for being a bad mother. She became addicted to prescription medications. My dad tried to keep things together, but eventually it was too much for him too. My parents divorced. My brother and sister blamed me for destroying the family. I can't blame them; it's true. But since then I've been alone. None of them will talk to me. I'm dead to them. My mother died of an overdose six years ago.

"It's been a long road. It seemed like anytime I started to feel happiness, the memory of the Hayeses' deaths or my mother's death would rise up to smack me back down. Something would say to me, 'How can you be happy when they're in the ground?' I've wondered if God could ever forgive me.

"I don't know why I decided to go into law, maybe it was all the time I'd spent in court and working with lawyers, but I had an aptitude for it. I got the second highest LSAT score in the state of Utah. I focused all my energy on my career. I worked hard, not just to succeed, but because there was nothing else in my life. Deep inside what I was really trying to do was prove that I wasn't worthless.

"But no amount of success in my career could fill that hole inside me. It was always there. I never felt free to find joy until I met Olivia. That's when I decided I would find someone to spend my life with. I dated some, I didn't have any trouble getting women, but I suppose I felt like you did. I didn't think they could comprehend or love the real me.

"When I saw you in that elevator I was speechless. I knew you didn't recognize me, but I recognized you. I felt like, in some way, we were kindred spirits. After that I couldn't get you off my mind. I wanted to know you better."

"That's why you came up with the contract," I said.

He nodded. "It seemed like a safe way to get close without hurting anyone. But then I fell in love." He looked into my eyes. "It wasn't hard. You're very loveable."

I looked at him gratefully but didn't speak.

"I wanted to protect you," he said. "From the world and from your past. But I'm part of that past, so that meant protecting you from me as well. I know I should have told you, but the timing never seemed right. And the stronger my feelings grew, the more afraid I was of losing you. And I had my own secret I didn't know how to share. In a way, I was fighting the same demon you were—deep inside I wondered whether you would reject me too if you knew the real me."

"I'm sorry I left you," I said. "You've had enough abandonment from those you loved." My voice fell with shame. "You didn't need it from me." I looked down for a moment as the emotion of the moment filled me. Then I looked back up into his eyes. "Could you still love me?"

It seemed an eternity that we gazed into each other's eyes, and then Nicholas came over to me and we embraced. Then we kissed. Passionately. Honestly. Completely. For the first time we kissed without masks. When our lips finally parted, I whispered, "I want to renew the contract."

He didn't speak for a moment. Then he said, "It's got to be a different contract."

"Different?"

He leaned back to look into my eyes. "We need to change the expiration date."

"To what?" I asked.

"In perpetuity."

I laughed. "You sound like such a lawyer."

"I am," he replied. "And no more platonic clause. It's definitely not going to be platonic."

A wide smile crossed my lips. "No," I said. "It's definitely not going to be platonic." I looked deep into his eyes. "In perpetuity?"

He nodded. "This time you really are signing your soul away."

I looked at him for a moment before I said, "All right, Mr. Lawyer. Got a pen?"

# Epilogue

*It should not surprise us that,
at the end of a journey, our destination
looks different than we imagined
at the beginning. Everything
looks different up close.*

## ELISE DUTTON'S DIARY

Nicholas and I were married the next spring in a small Italian village called Greve, nineteen miles south of Florence, in the Chianti wine district. It was a very small wedding, which was what we wanted. My sister, Cosette, and her husband, Ron, came. From the law firm there were Alan and Careen McKay and Scott and Sharon Hitesman. From ICE, Zoey was there. She financially swung the trip by talking Mark out of some of his frequent-flier miles. Not surprisingly, she's now carrying on a long-distance romance with an Italian guy named Dario.

The biggest surprise of our wedding day was the arrival of Nicholas's sister, Sheridan. She came without telling him. And she came to forgive. I don't think his joy could have been more full. To this day it's one of the few times I've seen Nicholas cry. We still have hopes that his brother might someday forgive him as well. We don't expect it, but we hope.

After our wedding, we honeymooned for two weeks in Rome and Sorrento and on Capri and the Amalfi coast, eventually flying back to the United States from Naples. When we got back to our home in Utah, there was a special wedding gift waiting for me—a Lladró of Cinderella and her pumpkin carriage. It was perfect. Maybe the figurine was really for Nicholas, but it doesn't matter. The story is mine.

I no longer work at ICE. I quit two months after I found out I was pregnant. I'm due next February, coincidentally the same month my Hannah was born.

Life is good. I'd be lying if I said that I had stopped being haunted by ghosts or trying myself in the court of regret. But things are different. The judge and jury are more merciful. After all these years, they are willing to listen to reason. And in court I'm no longer arguing my case alone. I found myself a pretty good lawyer.

# About the Author

Richard Paul Evans is the #1 best-selling author of *The Christmas Box*. Each of his more than twenty-five novels has been a *New York Times* bestseller. There are more than 20 million copies of his books in print worldwide, translated into more than twenty-four languages. He is the recipient of numerous awards, including the American Mothers Book Award, the *Romantic Times* Best Women's Novel of the Year Award, the German Audience Gold Award for Romance, three Religion Communicators Council Wilbur Awards, *The Washington Times* Humanitarian of the Century Award, and the Volunteers of America National Empathy Award. He lives in Salt Lake City, Utah, with his wife, Keri, and their five children. You can learn more about Richard on Facebook at www.facebook.com/RPEfans, or visit his website, www.richardpaulevans.com.

**Center Point Large Print**
600 Brooks Road / PO Box 1
Thorndike, ME 04986-0001 USA

(207) 568-3717

US & Canada:
1 800 929-9108
www.centerpointlargeprint.com